All rights reserved

The characters and events portrayed in this book are fictitious. Any similarity to real persons, living or dead, is coincidental and not intended by the author.

No part of this book may be reproduced, or stored in a retrieval system, or transmitted in any form or by any means, electronic, mechanical, photocopying, recording, or otherwise, without express written permission of the publisher.

ISBN: 9798343325782

Cover design by: S.G. Morand
Editing by: Jo Morand

Printed in the United States of America

This book is dedicated to Room 7, my amazing roommates who encouraged me in my writing, Joy Foster, Grace Pickens, and Ava Olsson. I look forward to reading your books someday. You guys are the best.

THE WORDS LEFT BEHIND

S. G. Morand

S. G. MORAND

CHAPTER 1

Perhaps the greatest trial of human existence is boredom.

For those who survive by busyness, driven by a need for accomplishment and the thrill of success, boredom is like an incurable disease, eating away at everything and driving the affected to a sort of unreasonable madness. Abigail Sinclair was not accustomed to boredom. She'd spent her entire life, pushing towards an unreachable goal. She pressed herself beyond her limits and beyond the expectations of others. Thus, she was always busy, always reaching for further goals, always shunning boredom. But things had changed recently. Her studies as a physician were nearing their end. One of the final acts on the stage of her dream was to exhibit her abilities in the field of an internship. She'd dreaded her mentor for some time, a private detective named Carlyle, a strange, unorthodox man. However, Abigail had come to appreciate Carlyle and his methods. She'd had her fair share of excitement working with him and reluctant as she might be to admit it, she had learned much. However, she had come to discover that one of the key tasks of a detective was to wait. Abigail hated waiting.

She spent many an afternoon sitting in the parlor of Carlyle's small apartment, staring longingly at the door and hoping that a case would present itself. She would have thought she would be grateful for the quiet after the events of the last case she had worked with Carlyle on. Instead, she was filled with a jittery impatience, made worse by the fact that there was so much going on in the world around her. The war raged on, men fought and died, and she could do nothing but wait anxiously for letters from her friend Arthur, confirming that he was still alive and well. Throughout the sojourn of silence, Abigail succeeded in whittling her fingernails, plucking out eyelashes, and rereading the same two paragraphs of her anatomy textbook eighty-nine times.

She felt like she was slowly going out of her mind. Meanwhile, Carlyle seemed totally unaffected by the solitude. He read through a few books, took long, leisurely walks along the quayside, and listened to the radio broadcasting news of the war. Detective Booker came to call a few times and tried to persuade Abigail and Carlyle to take dinner at his home. Carlyle refused the offers, saying he was much too busy to oblige. Abigail wished to be anywhere but the apartment. The few times when she went into her university for a change of scenery, she quickly changed her tune. She couldn't step foot on the campus without running into her professor which always ended in some type of confrontation. Abigail satisfied herself with sitting around and waiting. It was still better than the alternative of dealing with Professor Panet.

She spent some of her time reading the Bible Carlyle had given her and trying to understand it. The stories inside were sometimes too incredible to believe and sometimes unnervingly easy to accept. When Abigail asked Carlyle how anyone could believe that a man had been stuck in the belly of a great fish for three nights, he warned her that if she wanted to believe some of what was in the Bible then she had to believe it all.

"Nothing can be added or taken away," he told her. "If Jesus was dead for three days and rose again which is the basis of that belief, then a man could be in a fish's stomach for that amount of time. There is simply no give or take."

Abigail found it difficult to accept but she kept reading, having no better use for her time.

One afternoon as she was staring at her textbook until the words lost all shape and meaning, pondering why 'aorta' was composed of such a specific assortment of letters and sounds, there was a knock at the door. Abigail glanced up and met

Carlyle's eyes.

"A case?" she asked eagerly, pleadingly.

Carlyle stood and approached the door.

The knocking grew louder, more impatient. Abigail set her book aside and stood. It wasn't the knock of Detective Booker or the irritable landlord. No, this was someone new, maybe seeking Carlyle's help.

When the door fell open, Abigail was met with one person she never would have expected.

"Mother?" Abigail said in horror and surprise.

Mrs. Joan Sinclair was an elegant woman with pristine clothes, hair curled to perfection, and a stern, unyielding expression on her face.

"Abigail," Mrs. Sinclair coldly greeted.

Carlyle stood transfixed in surprise and indecision. "Please, come in, Madame," he finally said.

Mrs. Sinclair swept boldly into the room and Abigail fell a step back then another. She retreated from her mother's pursuit. Mrs. Sinclair had eyes fixed unflinchingly on Abigail. She paid no heed to Carlyle, the apartment, or anything except her daughter.

"Why are you here? How did you find me?" Abigail asked, her voice wavering a little, despite her best efforts to hide her unease. She thought of the letter she had received from her mother lying still unopened on her desk.

Mrs. Sinclair crossed her arms and glared. "It was no easy feat. I finally tracked you down to that disgraceful medical school. Then I was told you were away on an internship with a nobody detective of all things. Your father and I are ashamed of your behavior."

Abigail cringed at the words.

She could imagine her mother's outrage at first finding Abigail at a medical school, then at hearing she was working with a detective to investigate murders. Abigail could still see the fury etched into her mother's features. But Abigail had changed over the years and over the last month or so with Carlyle she had witnessed murder, arson, deceit, and all manners of wickedness. She found with surprise that her mother no longer scared her to such an extent as before. Her initial shock began to wear off. She knew her family would find her eventually. She knew confrontation was inevitable. She stood her ground, refusing to back one more step.

"Have you never considered, Mother, that maybe there was a reason I never told you and Father where I was going or what I intended to do?"

"I understand that you

wanted no one to interfere with your foolish scheme. To think that you planned all along to become a doctor. A doctor!"

"Is it so hard to believe that I'm capable of such a thing?"

"Quite frankly, yes."

Abigail was surprised at how much the words hurt. She'd always felt that her parents underestimated her abilities but she wouldn't have thought her mother would be so dismissive at what she had dreamed of achieving.

"Mrs. Sinclair," Carlyle interjected.

Abigail had nearly forgotten her mentor was there. She flushed with embarrassment, knowing that Carlyle was forced to witness her familial tussle.

"Mrs. Sinclair," Carlyle repeated, "my name is Carlyle, I'm the detective your daughter has been interning under in order to complete the requirements to obtain her medical license. I'm afraid I knew nothing of the situation and you have my apologies for any worry and confusion that may have been caused. However, I assure you that your daughter has been indispensable with her talents as a physician. Her actions while working with me have saved more than one life in a very short timeframe. She is more than capable of achieving her license and becoming a fully-fledged doctor."

Mrs. Sinclair huffed dismissively and ignored Carlyle. "I was willing to let you run off and never see your family again, Abigail. I guess it's my reward for raising you that you should treat your father and me in such a way. But things have changed now and it's time for you to give up your ridiculous scheme and come home."

Abigail laughed derisively. "You raised me, did you? You didn't raise. You were too enthralled in your own desires to care much for what I did as long as I never disappointed or embarrassed you. I'll never come home. You can leave now for all I care. I won't be going with you."

Mrs. Sinclair sighed and closed her eyes. Her face twisted into a pained expression as she attempted to restrain her temper. After a long, agonizing pause, she spoke, her words harsh and short. "Quincey has gone missing."

Abigail's heart lurched in her chest. She fell silent, all of the fight rushing out of her, the wind going out of her sails.

"W...what?" the words came out strangled.

"You must return home. Quincey is gone. You're all that we have left, at least until we find him."

"What do you mean Quincey's gone? Is he okay? Why did he leave? What's going on?"

Mrs. Sinclair lifted her chin defiantly, gathering her composure once more. "Much has changed while you've been gone, Abigail. There was no way to contact you to inform you of what was happening and why should we have. You made it perfectly clear that you wanted nothing more to do with any of us."

"That's not fair. Quincey's my brother. If something happened…"

"That's enough. What's done is done."

"But, what happened while I was gone? What's wrong?" Abigail pleaded, her heart hammering erratically in her chest. Something was seriously wrong, something more than just Quincey going missing, but what it was, Abigail had no idea.

"I'll inform you of everything later when you return home."

"You're going to bribe me with the information? I deserve to know! Besides, I can't just leave. I have my studies and my internship."

"I wasn't offering you an option, Abigail. You're coming with me. You've always been a rebellious child but it's time for you to grow up and abandon your ridiculous notion that you could ever be a doctor."

Abigail squared her shoulders, prepared to continue her fight but Carlyle took that moment to interrupt the conflict.

"I believe you can both be appeased," he said. "Things are quiet here but it seems there is a mystery waiting to be solved. A young man has gone missing, that is a mystery indeed. If you will accept, Madame, I am willing to freely offer my services to discover what happened to Quincey Sinclair."

Mrs. Sinclair truly took in Carlyle for the first time. She appraised the odd man like a vulture surveying a corpse in the desert.

"Well, Mr. Carlyle. I do not approve of my daughter's work with you but I am desperate. My son has gone missing and my daughter refuses to come home. It certainly wouldn't hurt to have a detective on the case, especially with everything else that has taken place, and if it is what it takes to persuade Abigail to return, then I will accept your offer."

"What else has happened?" Abigail asked, feeling her dread sour into despair.

Mrs. Sinclair ignored the question. "There is a train leaving from Chicago to Akron, Ohio in a few hours. I'll procure your ticket,

Mr. Carlyle, while you and Abigail pack your things. Please, meet me at the station as soon as possible."

She didn't say anything more to Abigail before she turned and left, slamming the door of the apartment closed behind her. Abigail turned on her heel and hurried to her room to gather her things, including the confusing Bible, before Carlyle could speak. She could only guess what her mentor would have to say and she didn't want to hear any of it. She thought of Quincey and her mother's cryptic clues that something was horribly amiss in Cleveland. Abigail wasn't much for praying but as she gathered her things, she found herself whispering pleas and hoping that God would hear.

CHAPTER 2

The train ride was silent, deafeningly so. Abigail sat next to Carlyle and across from her mother in the small compartment that had been rented for them. Abigail spent most of the ride determinedly staring out of the window so she didn't have to meet her mother's piercing glare head-on. Carlyle, always more self-contained and not one for small talk, maintained the silence without attempting to make conversation. At first, Abigail had tried to get her mother to explain what was wrong at home but Mrs. Sinclair was determined to keep quiet about everything until Abigail was safely ensconced in her family home. Abigail detested trains. The small area confined her to uncomfortable proximity with her mother and there was no escape for the long hours until they reached their destination.

The journey was uncomfortable but Abigail thought she might very well die of embarrassment when they stepped out of the train and found a shining black cherry convertible with gleaming chrome and a stag hood ornament waiting for them, driver included.

"I've never seen such a fine car," Carlyle commented, admiring the machine.

"It's a Packard 160 Convertible," Mrs. Sinclair announced proudly. "My husband is quite the connoisseur of fine automobiles."

Abigail looked at it with disgust. "A new toy for Father I see. Even with a war raging and men going overseas to die, he can find a way to flaunt his wealth."

Abigail's mother ignored her comment and allowed the driver to assist her into the car. As Abigail climbed in the back beside Carlyle, she mumbled, "Just wait. This car is nothing compared to the rest."

It was dark by the time the automobile pulled into the neighborhood.

"These houses are certainly grander than I had envisioned, Miss Abigail, when you told me you were from Ohio," Carlyle commented.

The whole neighborhood was filled with mansions of the most extravagant structures and designs. The estates stretched out over acres, sprawling like little cities complete with gardens and stables, servants' homes and garages.

"The sheer quantity is astounding," Carlyle said.

His voice mirrored how Abigail felt. So much luxury, so much excess, while so many others barely got by. The Depression had impacted so many and driven them to despair and want. Meanwhile, this haven of wealth had endured and prospered in its own private world, set apart.

Mrs. Sinclair nodded with pride, pleased at what she understood to be Carlyle's interest and awe at the beautiful opulence around. "Millionaire's Row is nothing to what it once was. After the Depression, many of the fine families in this area went bankrupt. They forfeited their pride and sold their estates to schools or boarding homes.

Some of the mansions were destroyed altogether," Mrs. Sinclair regretfully informed him. "Only a few of the most influential families remain and the Sinclairs are chief amongst them."

Abigail couldn't help but roll her eyes at the stark exaggeration. Carlyle gave her a questioning look but she didn't respond to his unspoken question. They drove past the mansions with their long, paved approaches, towering, turreted walls, windows lit from within like a million flickering candles, and chimneys poking out like fingers pointing to the heavens.

Abigail watched Carlyle's reaction as they approached the elegant Sinclair estate. It really couldn't be done justice to describe it in the dark. When the sun shone on the bright stones, the whole place seemed to glow. Even the vines creeping up the face of the mansion sprang to new life. The mansion was so large it blotted out the moon in the sky. It towered above with large windows designed like those of a cathedral, spired peak, regal columns and arches, and carvings etched into the stone. The approach was all green lawns and trees, nature meeting architecture in a beautiful embrace. The driveway was long and curved, paved with stones like a medieval courtyard. The driver honked the horn of the vehicle to urge a stag that had wandered onto the path away. The stag paused and studied the automobile and its passengers. His antlers and regal bearing made Abigail feel small and insignificant. He moved along, unhurried, unbothered, and the car lurched forward once again. It pulled to a stop under the carriage arch, electric lights illuminating the dark sky.

Abigail glanced once again

slackened with confusion. "Who is this?"

Abigail released a breath of relief at the attention being focused away from her. The respite, no matter how brief, was a welcome one.

"My name is Carlyle, I'm a private detective. I have also been acting as the mentor for your daughter's internship. Your wife has graciously accepted the offer of my free services to aid in solving the disappearance of your son."

Mr. Sinclair blinked once, twice, then cleared his throat. "Well, Mr. Carlyle, please excuse my behavior just now. It's a pleasure to meet you and I thank you sincerely for your offer to help us during this trying time."

Abigail had to look away to hide her disgust. She shouldn't have been surprised. Her parents were experts at shifting their demeanors in an instant to save face and ensure they were seen in a favorable light. Mr. and Mrs. Sinclair had a reputation to uphold after all. Her father's apologies and thanks were paper-thin, shallow things that could be revoked just as quickly as they had been instated.

Carlyle nodded cordially and shook Mr. Sinclair's hand but Abigail noticed with relief that he didn't seem fooled by the act of gratitude or the kind greeting. Carlyle was perceptive, it was a natural trait of detectives and one that Abigail noticed her mentor had a special talent for. She was grateful that he wasn't as easily won over as others might be.

"Please, come into the parlor," Mr. Sinclair said, gesturing the way. "Now that *Abigail* has *finally* returned, there is much to be discussed. That's the ticket daughter of mine, if you leave, there is much we are no longer obligated to make you privy to.

A lot has happened since your departure."

"So I've heard," Abigail finally ventured to speak, unable to fully smother her annoyance. "Obviously whatever it was wasn't important enough to make me return. You knew that the only way I would ever step foot in this house again was because of Quincey."

Suddenly a horrible thought occurred to Abigail. She halted and couldn't keep the anxiety out of her tone when she asked, "Is Quincey even gone, or did you just say as much to force me back here?"

Abigail had scarcely gotten the words out when Mr. Sinclair snapped. He whirled on her, breaking off any further statement with his simple words, "Fitz Sawyer is dead."

No. No, no, no. Not Fitz, surely not, but maybe. It was possible of course, probable even. If it was anyone, it would have been Fitz, reckless, childish, self-centered, Fitz. Her friend... once, or rather Quincey's friend.

"What?" Abigail asked in shock. "How?"

"There was an accident," Mrs. Sinclair said, not unkindly. "Fitz and Merit were walking along the cliffs and Fitz fell. It happened about a month ago. We wanted to tell you, Abigail, but we had no way of contacting you."

"You should have tried harder!"

"You forfeited your right to know when you ran away," Mr. Sinclair said coldly.

Abigail's temper rose hot and fast. "Fitz was my friend!"

Mr. Sinclair snorted in amusement at the statement. "You humor yourself, Abigail. Fitz was Quincey's friend, never yours."

Abigail bristled at the words but didn't argue further. Another part of the news sunk in at that moment. She paled as her mind latched onto the information and understood how awful things truly were. "Merit."

Mrs. Sinclair sighed, sharing Abigail's worry. "Yes, Merit is understandably not taking it well. He blames himself for what happened on the cliffs."

"As he should," Mr. Sinclair said with animosity. "It was his fault that the accident occurred. Strange boy as he's always been and with the shadow of death following his every step. He brings death wherever he goes. I knew he was no good and I dearly wish that uncle of his would have taken him from this neighborhood long ago. Maybe then, none of this would have happened."

"None of this could have possibly been Merit's fault," Abigail argued.

"Poor Lizzy is handling it all with grace," Mrs. Sinclair

said, wringing her hands together, "even though Fitz was her fiancé."

"Fiancé?" Abigail wondered if she'd misheard.

"Oh, I thought you knew that much. I suppose that was after you left as well," Mrs. Sinclair said carelessly. "Lizzy came to live year-round with her aunt and uncle two winters ago. The girl always wanted to be here and begged her parents to let her stay even after the summer was over but it wasn't until she was done with school that they finally consented. Well, as soon as she was here permanently, she and Fitz fell into a whirlwind romance. I suppose it's to be expected seeing as they grew up together. I had always hoped Lizzy might choose Quincey but Fitz was a strapping young man after all. They were to be married later this summer. But now…"

Abigail didn't know what to say. Fitz and Lizzy. It didn't surprise her, not really. Abigail, Quincey, Fitz, Lizzy, and Merit, they had grown up together, the children of Millionaire's Row. Lizzy had always been the star of their group, the boys doted on her, and Abigail wanted to be her. Abigail had always suspected one of the three boys would end up with Lizzy. It was no shock that Fitz, competitive as he had always been, had won that particular competition.

"What about Quincey? Where is he? Why did he leave? Fitz was his best friend; he must have been heartbroken." Abigail thought of Quincey with a pang in her heart. He and Fitz had been inseparable, closer than any of the rest of them.

"Quincey left right after Fitz's death," Mr. Sinclair said, stepping towards a side table and pouring himself a glass of bourbon.

Abigail saw Carlyle stiffen

out of the corner of her eye. She wondered what he was thinking.

"Do you know of anything that could have prompted Quincey's departure?" Carlyle asked.

"Well, he was of course upset over Fitz's death, especially because they had a fight before Fitz's accident," Mrs. Sinclair said.

"Quincey had been acting differently for months preceding the accident," Mr. Sinclair explained.

"Do you remember when this strange behavior began?" Carlyle pressed.

"About the time Abigail ran away," Mr. Sinclair said, glaring at his daughter. "In fact, I suspect it was her fault that Quincey changed so severely. He became dreadfully serious and he pushed everyone close to him away."

"He was terribly upset when Abigail left," Mrs. Sinclair told

Carlyle. "He refused to talk to anyone about it. He fought with us constantly and even with his friends, not just Quincey but Merit and Lizzy too."

Abigail felt her mouth go dry. Her vision swam a little with the weight of everything that had happened. Fitz was dead and Quincey was gone. She thought of the last time she had seen Quincey, the things she had said. Had some of this been her fault? And Fitz was dead. Dead! Abigail felt sick. Her shoulders hunched. She wanted to be far, far away from her parents. She wanted to be alone.

"I assure you, Mr. and Mrs. Sinclair, I will do everything I can to help find your son," Carlyle said.

Abigail turned and abruptly strode out of the room. Her mother's demands for her to return fell on deaf ears. Abigail took the stairs to her old room two at a time, desperate to escape. She had to find Quincey. She had to get out of the house and away from her family as soon as possible. Abigail's mind grasped desperately for a solution, a way to solve the problem. She had a problem and she needed to find some way to solve it. There had to be something she could do, some way she could make things right. She was a doctor, or she would be soon, she was supposed to fix things.

First, she would speak to Merit and Lizzy. She would find out every last detail of what really happened. Then, she would find a solution from there. She didn't doubt that there was some solution, a way to bring Quincey back, there always was an answer if one looked hard enough.

Abigail opened the door to her old room and was staggered by the mixed feeling of nostalgia and suffocation. It was as if she were stepping into a gilded cage.

and Lizzy. Abigail had planned to escape without anyone's notice but when she descended the stairs, she found Carlyle already awake and waiting for her. She supposed she shouldn't have been surprised. While working with him, she had learned that he was an early riser, the type of person who hated to waste a morning. He held a mug of coffee out to her as she approached. Abigail gladly took it. She hadn't slept well. Her childhood bedroom had filled her mind with strange, unsettling dreams, not to mention the bed was more cramped now that she was grown.

"If you intend to speak to your old friends, it's likely too early," Carlyle told her. "Few are awake at this hour if they can help it."

Abigail wondered how he had known what she was planning. Carlyle always had a way of seeing the hidden side of things and hearing the unspoken claims.

"I know," she agreed. "But I can't stand to be in this house any longer. I have to get outside."

"Then, might I suggest you give me a tour of the estate grounds, Miss Abigail. I'm intrigued by the place and I believe having an idea of the layout of the property may be useful in discovering what became of your brother."

Abigail readily agreed. Taking her coffee outside with her, knowing her mother would be outraged at her fine China leaving the house, Abigail began to lead Carlyle around the estate.

"The estate is called Stag Hall for obvious reasons," Abigail told him, gesturing to the antlered stags that wandered the grounds, grazing on the immaculately green lawns. "My first foray as a doctor was when Fitz and Quinn tried to mount and ride two of the bucks.

Like most boys their age, they frequently got into trouble and to make matters worse they believed they were untouchable because of their wealth. As I'm sure you can surmise, their attempt to ride the beasts failed miserably. Fitz was practically impaled by the antlers and Quinn was scratched up from a bad fall. I took it upon myself to patch them up before help could arrive and I offered them a pretty stern scolding along with it."

Carlyle gave a short snort of amusement. "Yes, that seems a fitting start to your illustrious career."

Abigail grinned but the smile quickly faded. "There are so many memories attached to this place. I hate being back here."

"I have found that try as you might you can never run from the past forever," Carlyle told her. "Sometimes it is necessary to face it in order to look to the future."

Maybe he was right but Abigail still didn't like it. The estate was exactly as she remembered it. It was as if nothing had changed. It was unsettling and eerie. The grounds were the same, her family was the same. The past was alive and well in this secluded little world.

"I'm sorry I didn't tell you about any of this," Abigail told Carlyle. "You never should have been dragged into this mess."

Carlyle was silent a moment and Abigail feared he would tell her he had decided to return to Chicago, leaving her here. Finally, he spoke.

"There are parts of ourselves we wish no one had to know. You know the circumstances that led me to my path as a private detective. You know that I tell few people of those events," Carlyle said.

Abigail remembered the

night after they had saved Jack Davis from death when she and Carlyle had kept vigil the whole night, unable to sleep. She remembered the story of the life Carlyle had been unable to save, the mistakes he had made, and his own brush with death that had led his first assistant Dr. Hastings to leave his service.

"This is hardly comparable to that," Abigail said. "Part of the reason you kept quiet about everything was to protect Dr. Hastings. There's no reason why I should have hidden all of this. I'm just... I'm ashamed of it all, of their behavior, of this wealth squandered, of my cowardice in fleeing from it."

"Abigail," Carlyle said softly, "you chose to create your own life, a life that you didn't have to be ashamed of. You were under no obligation to tell me or anyone else about your past. It was a shock to be sure when your mother appeared unexpectedly but none of this takes away from who you are, a brave, determined physician with a heart for others and a mind that rivals the best in your field."

Abigail blushed at the praise. She knew that Carlyle didn't bestow it lightly. "I am sorry for bringing you into this mess," she said, changing the subject.

Carlyle shrugged. "You rescued me from the boredom of waiting, that's all. There is a mystery here and I intend to solve it. A young man had gone missing and I intend to find out why. Now, please tell me more about this illustrious property."

Abigail led her mentor through the estate pointing out other landmarks on the property. "My father had this estate built when he was young. He gained his wealth as an automobile magnate, which is part of the reason he has such expensive taste in vehicles. When the Great Depression hit, many families in this area went bankrupt and had to sell their homes or abandon them altogether. Stag Hall is one of the few remaining mansions in the area. My father was fortunate enough to have invested in a newspaper company in addition to his automobile manufacturing. It was tough getting by for a while but there is always news to be had and so his company survived and so did his wealth for the most part. After the Depression, he gained a government contract to manufacture parts for tanks and other equipment, I suspect any wealth he lost during the Depression he has regained twofold now."

Abigail led Carlyle towards the back of the house where a large patio stretched out in front of a section of the manor that boasted huge windows which revealed an empty ballroom beyond. "This is the ballroom. My father used to throw extravagant parties even during the Depression. The parties drew people from the best families all around the country and helped preserve our family's status. It helped that a good friend of my father's was a bootlegger who always ensured the parties were overflowing with champagne and other illicit beverages. That always served to draw in a crowd."

"It was no different in Chicago during that time," Carlyle told her. "Even in times of great distress, the drink and the dance readily flowed. People turned to excess and vice when they should have turned to God."

Abigail turned away from the ballroom, remembering the nights of deafening noise and drunkenness that had kept her awake when all she wanted was to sleep and escape. She had always been disgusted with the life her parents lived. Maybe that was why the teachings of Jesus that she had read in the Bible were somewhat appealing and she couldn't outright cast them aside. A life lived in the pursuit of love, faith, and purity was so in contrast to the childhood Abigail had been exposed to. Deep down she wanted that kind of life but she wasn't sure if she could accept the route to achieve it.

"My father wanted a perfect family to demonstrate his perfect wealth and influence," Abigail told Carlyle. "He married a rich woman from an important family and then they had two children a boy and a girl. Quincey was raised to inherit, brought up as a miniature version of our father, sent to boarding school, and made to stand at our father's side during all of the important events.

And I was confined to the house and neighborhood given lessons from the best tutors in French, Latin, piano, and literature. I liked science the best much to my parents' dismay. When I was twelve one of my instructors gave me an anatomy textbook. I knew my mother wouldn't approve so I hid the book. I treasured it and became obsessed with the pursuit of medicine. I watched the parties that mocked the suffering of so many and I knew I wanted to help people instead of laughing at their misery."

Abigail shook her head to clear her thoughts. She led Carlyle away from the house. She gestured to a tree-enshrouded path and explained, "There's a pond down among the trees where we used to swim as children."

Abigail didn't lead Carlyle to the pond. She had no wish to see that place ever again. She pushed onward until they were standing at the beginning of a dirt pathway. "This is the path to the cliffside," Abigail said flatly.

She stood on the path and willing her legs to move forward. She knew that the cliffs were the one place where she and Carlyle most needed to investigate. It was the place where Fitz had died. Carlyle would want to see the area. He would want to look for hints of what had happened. But Abigail couldn't bring herself to move. She didn't want to see evidence of Fitz's death. Carlyle must have sensed her unease at the idea of walking that path because he cleared his throat.

"We'll wait to investigate until later, Miss Abigail."

Abigail sighed in relief and stepped off of the path willingly. She blinked a few times as if awakening from a trance and then headed back towards the manor.

"This place may appear beautiful at first glance but I've seen the darker side of it more often than not. My brother and I used to refer to Stag Hall as the Glass Castle. It was shining and captivating from the outside but the inside was cold and pristine. If one looked hard enough they could see the cracks."

"Were you and your brother close?" Carlyle asked her.

"Yes, once."

Abigail looked at the sky and realized the sun had risen. "We should head to Merit's estate. He's always had an erratic sleep schedule so he might be up early."

Abigail led the way along a pathway until they reached the grounds of an estate even more spectacular than the Sinclair mansion. Raleighdom was a grand house of extravagant proportions and architecture. If Stag Hall was impressive then Raleighdom was awe-inspiring. Carlyle stood admiring the structure with its expansive grounds for a long moment.

"This estate must belong to a very wealthy family," Carlyle finally remarked.

"Not quite," Abigail explained. "It's all Merit's."

Carlyle raised an eyebrow in surprise and disbelief. "It's impressive that such a young man would possess such a great fortune."

Abigail shrugged. "It's his inheritance. Merit lost his father in the First World War. His mother died of pneumonia when he was a boy. He was left to the care of his nursemaids. His only living relative is an estranged uncle in Poland."

"Such a unique upbringing must make for a very interesting young man."

"I suppose that's a fitting word to describe Merit. Even with such a tumultuous childhood, he was always the calmest of our group. He was a thinker. He had a way with words and wrote the most amazing poetry even as a child. I think without him Quinn and Fitz probably would have gotten themselves hurt much worse."

Abigail was eager to see Merit. She'd always felt a greater connection to him than she had to Fitz or even Quinn at times. She worried about how he was handling Fitz's death though.

"Merit has always been more... sensitive than the other boys. With all of the death he's already experienced, I worry about how he's taking things after Fitz..."

Carlyle nodded in understanding and followed Abigail up the path to Merit's home.

Abigail paused at the door, her hand reaching to knock. She

turned back to Carlyle. "One more thing, when you meet Merit, he's... well, you'll see."

CHAPTER 4

A servant opened the door for them, a new member of the household whom Abigail didn't recognize.

"Hello, my name is Abigail Sinclair," Abigail introduced herself, "and my companion here is Mr. Carlyle. We've come to speak to Merit."

"Mr. Raleigh isn't taking visitors at the moment," the servant announced. "May I take your card?"

Abigail peered over the

man's shoulder into the house, it was quiet and empty. "Is Mrs. Trenton here?" Abigail asked. She remembered the old housekeeper, the kind woman who had practically raised Merit.

"Mrs. Trenton is no longer in the service of this household," the servant explained.

Abigail shook her head. "No, that can't be right. Merit would never dismiss her."

The servant sighed. "May I take your card miss?"

Abigail was about to force her way into the home when she heard a familiar voice. "Abigail, is that you?"

"Lizzy," Abigail exhaled the name like a breath of relief.

Lizzy appeared and shooed the servant away, gesturing for Abigail and Carlyle to enter the house.

"Oh Abigail, you have no idea how relieved I am to see you,"

Lizzy said, pulling Abigail into an embrace.

Abigail felt the tell-tale dampness of tears falling on her shoulders. "Lizzy, what's wrong?" Abigail knew what was wrong though and she regretted the words as soon as they left her mouth.

"Do you know everything?" Lizzy asked, pulling away and sucking in deep breaths to calm herself. She wiped at her eyes, trying to compose herself.

"I do, or at least what my parents have told me. I came to see Merit in hopes that he could fill in the blanks."

"Well, I wish you the best of luck at that. I've been trying to get in to see Merit since dawn and I've been doing the same for the past two days. He's locked himself in his office and refuses to see anyone, even me. Merit blames himself for the accident. He's been inconsolable ever since Fitz died." Lizzy choked on the word.

Abigail rubbed Lizzy's shoulder reassuringly. "I'm so sorry, Lizzy. I heard that you were engaged. I should have been here."

Lizzy shook her head. "There's nothing you could have done. I'm just glad you're here now. I've been trying my best to get Merit to talk but he's just become more and more reserved, especially around me. Now, with Quinn disappearing, he's only gotten worse."

Lizzy led them further into the house towards Merit's office. The inside of Merit's estate was just as breathtaking as the exterior. Wood coffered ceilings, leather upholstered furniture, rich burgundy wallpaper, winding staircases with red carpet runners, herringbone patterned floors, and renaissance-style paintings decorating every wall. The difference of Merit's home from the Sinclair estate was the clear decision to seek beauty and elegance over meaningless excess. The Raleigh home was filled with art, the finest architectural design, and reminders of Merit's Polish heritage. But it was lacking personal touches. Like Abigail's childhood home, Merit's estate was untouched but it had always been that way. After his parents had died, he'd kept every detail of the home the same. There were few signs of Merit in the expansive structure. Abigail knew that only his office and room held any personal touches. It was more like a museum than a home.

As they walked, Carlyle extended a hand to Lizzy and introduced himself. "I am Detective Carlyle. Miss Abigail has been conducting her medical internship under my tutelage and now I've volunteered my services to investigate Quincey Sinclair's disappearance."

"Oh, I've been dreadfully rude haven't I," Lizzy fretted. "My name is Elizabeth Sutton, Lizzy for short. You must forgive me, Mr. Carlyle, it's just I've been so scattered with everything that's happened."

"No need for apologies, Miss Sutton. I hope you don't mind my asking but your accent..."

Lizzy laughed. "I guess it sticks out around here, doesn't it? I'm from Georgia originally. That's where my parents live. My aunt and uncle have a mansion here that I've stayed at every summer since I was eight. It's only recently that I've begun to stay here year-round. I fear that's when everything began to fall apart."

"That's not true, Lizzy. You told me there's nothing I could have done and I'll tell you the same," Abigail assured her friend.

Lizzy didn't respond, she looked away as if she didn't believe Abigail's claim.

"I'm happy you're here Mr. Carlyle but I admit that I'm a little concerned at the fact that a detective has been involved in everything," Lizzy said.

"Quincey's gone missing, Lizzy, Carlyle might be the only one who can find him," Abigail said.

Lizzy brushed off the statement. "I'm sure Quinn left entirely of his own volition. He's been acting strange since you left, Abigail. He acted as if he were disgusted with all of us. It was like he was an entirely different person. I don't see any reason to involve a detective in what seems to be Quinn's own hardheadedness."

Abigail wanted to argue further but she didn't bother. Lizzy always got her way. She always had. If she had made up her mind about something, there was no persuading her otherwise. Abigail was reminded suddenly of all of the times she had clashed with Lizzy and why she hadn't made an effort to keep in touch with her friend when she left for medical school.

"I need to talk to Merit," Abigail said, brushing away Lizzy's thoughtless words. "I won't take no for an answer."

She approached Merit's office, a familiar room. She remembered sitting on the floor beside the oaken desk with Lizzy and Quinn while Merit paced the room berating an unrepentant Fitz for his latest foolishness. She remembered long nights when Merit would be bent over the desk, working tirelessly at his poems, the rest of them gathered around with hot cocoa, playing cards and joking.

Abigail approached the office with a mixed feeling of

excitement and trepidation. It had been so long since she'd last seen Merit. She was eager to see him again but she was nervous too. Lizzy said he had isolated himself. How bad were things? Abigail feared the answer.

Abigail took a deep breath and pounded relentlessly on the door. "Merit, it's Abigail Sinclair, open up!"

The door opened a crack and Merit peered out with bleary, red-rimmed eyes. "Abigail?"

His voice was soft, her name barely spoken. Merit's tone was tinged with surprise and unbelief. "What are you doing here?"

"Hello, Merit. May I come in?"

Merit hesitated before sighing and stepping back to allow Abigail and the others entrance into his office. As the group entered, Merit turned pointedly away from Lizzy, refusing to acknowledge her presence. He paid no attention whatsoever to Carlyle.

Abigail couldn't help but notice the pitiful state Merit was in. He was thin, his face drawn tight over too sharp cheekbones and his reddened eyes shadowed by eyebrows pinched together in concern. Merit looked so unfamiliar to Abigail that she doubted for a moment she was looking at the same boy she had known. A change had happened in Merit. Abigail suspected it had begun before Fitz's death.

"Mr. Raleigh, I am Detective Carlyle," Carlyle introduced.

He didn't have the chance to say anything further. Merit's shoulders stiffened and Abigail saw the first real sign of life from his. A fire sparked behind his lifeless eyes and he looked at Carlyle eagerly.

"A detective? Yes, good, that's good. You've come to

investigate Fitz's death. I was wondering when someone would come."

"What? No, Carlyle is here to look into Quinn's disappearance," Abigail explained. "Why would someone need to investigate Fitz's death? It was an accident. Wasn't it?"

A strange look came over Merit's face that Abigail couldn't decipher.

"Merit, don't," Lizzy warned.

"Stay out of this, Elizabeth!" Merit snapped.

Abigail recoiled in shock. Merit never called Lizzy by her full name, none of them did. Lizzy only frowned; her eyes were hard. She crossed her arms over her chest and looked away.

"Fitz was murdered," Merit said.

Abigail felt like a projectile had pierced into her chest. "That's... no that can't be true."

Lizzy shook her head. "That's what I've been trying to tell him. It was an accident, Merit. An *accident*."

"Why do you believe it to be a murder, Mr. Raleigh?" Carlyle asked. There was no hint of derision or disbelief in his tone.

Merit looked relieved. "You believe me then, Mr. Carlyle? You believe he was murdered too?"

"I do not come to conclusions without all of the proof," Carlyle explained. "You were with the young man when he died, yes, I expect you know more about what happened than any of us."

Merit swallowed hard and nodded.

"Then, please, tell us everything," Carlyle urged.

Merit sunk into his desk chair and placed his elbows on the great wooden desk. The position made Abigail realize how much older he looked from the last time she had seen him.

"It was supposed to be a normal walk. Fitz was stressed and I knew he needed to blow off some steam. I suggested we go to the cliffs so he could get some fresh air away from the neighborhood. We had walked the path countless times before. I never thought… I never thought there could be any danger in it. He walked to the edge of the cliff. I was watching him when suddenly he was just… gone. The whole cliffside had cracked. Fitz fell before I could even think to save him. Nothing like that had ever happened before. I knew that someone must have chiseled out a piece of the cliff face so it would collapse as soon as Fitz stepped foot on it."

"But who would want Fitz dead?" Abigail asked.

Merit gave her a knowing look. "You know as well as I do

that Fitz was difficult. There were plenty of people who might have wanted him gone."

"That's a terrible thing to say, Merit," Lizzy exclaimed, her voice high-pitched with anger and fear. "We all loved Fitz. No one would wish him dead."

Merit glared at her and a conversation seemed to pass between them. Lizzy averted her eyes.

"If someone did chisel out the cliffside, then they could have just as easily been targeting *you*, Merit," Lizzy argued. "You are the heir to millions and the only family who would miss you is an uncle who is impossible to contact. Someone could have concocted a plan to claim your fortune."

"No, I'm sure Fitz was the target, not me."

"You're being unreasonable, Merit!"

Merit ignored her.

Lizzy paled and clutched at her chest as if her heart had skipped a beat. "Oh, God," she exclaimed. "What if Quincey did it?"

"What? No!" Abigail refuted immediately. "What are you talking about, Lizzy? Quinn and Fitz were best friends. Quinn would never kill anyone and especially not Fitz."

Lizzy looked at her pityingly, "Oh, Abigail, Quinn changed while you were gone. You have no idea how often he and Fitz fought, terrible fights too. They hated each other at the end. In fact, Quinn and Fitz had a particularly awful fight right before the accident. That's why Quinn didn't go with Merit and Fitz to the cliffside."

"The fight was because of you," Merit reminded Lizzy.

She recoiled as if he had struck her. "No." she shook her

head in dismissal.

"Quinn fought Fitz because of how he saw him treating you, Lizzy. I wish I had been brave enough to fight Fitz like Quinn did."

"Did Fitz hurt you, Lizzy?" Abigail asked, horrified.

"It was nothing," Lizzy said firmly. "Quinn was being overly dramatic about everything. But I fear he might have lost his temper and killed Fitz. That would explain why he disappeared. He ran away so no one would make him pay for his crimes."

Abigail looked at Carlyle with mounting horror. No, it couldn't be possible that Quinn had killed Fitz. Abigail knew her brother, didn't she? She remembered how reckless Quinn had been when she left. She remembered part of the reason *why* she left. Carlyle's face spoke volumes. His eyes were downcast and a thoughtful expression was on his face. He suspected the same, she realized. She recalled how concerned he had looked when Fitz's death had been revealed and her mother had told them that Quinn ran away soon after.

"You believe her," Abigail stated to Carlyle with horror.

Carlyle met Abigail's gaze head-on. "I'll look into all of this. I cannot believe anything until I've gathered all of the facts. It may have been only an accident as was originally expected."

Merit put his head in his hands and pulled at his hair. "It was a murder. I know it was."

"Merit," Lizzy said reassuringly. She reached to place a hand on his shoulder and he flinched.

He jerked his head up, glaring. "Get out, all of you! Leave me alone!"

Carlyle ushered them

hurriedly out of the room. Abigail allowed herself to be escorted away in a daze. She heard Carlyle's soft, careful words as he walked with her back to Stag Hall.

"There could have been any number of reasons for your brother to disappear, Miss Abigail. Please do not concern yourself too much with what Miss Sutton suggested. However, I urge you also to keep an open mind. I regretfully suspect that you haven't entirely ruled out Quincey's involvement in all of this. Do you have a reason for suspecting that Quincey might be involved in this?"

Abigail snapped out of her daze long enough to consider Carlyle's question. She didn't want to voice the words but she still spoke, her voice flat and lifeless. "The last time I saw my brother, he was irritable, reckless, and extravagant in his vices. He was too much like Fitz and my father. Everyone says he changed but I can't help but wonder if he changed for the better or the worse."

CHAPTER 5

When they had left Merit's house and bid their farewells to Lizzy who was determined to stay and attempt to get Merit to talk further, Carlyle told Abigail, "It's time to investigate the cliffs."

Abigail dreaded stepping foot on that cursed land. She dreaded to see the place where Fitz had fallen but she knew it was necessary if they were to get to the bottom of this. With Quinn a suspect, Abigail was more determined to find out what happened to Fitz than ever before.

"If you would prefer, I can go alone," Carlyle offered.

"No, as much as I'd like to avoid it, I need to go and see it for myself."

It wasn't difficult to find the spot of the accident. The cliffside walk posed no real trail, only a beaten-down path through dirt and rocks. Abigail knew the path well enough and it was clear where the cliff had broken away. The concave recess left behind by a fallen ledge and the small, fragmented rocks scattered all around were evidence enough of the cliff giving way. Abigail and Carlyle approached the broken ledge and looked down to the rocky valley below. Rocks both small and large were spread at the base, evidence of the fallen ledge. Abigail cringed at the sight of something red splattered among the stones. She pulled away from the cliff edge, leaving Carlyle to investigate further. He knelt at the edge and carefully examined the concave edge of the cliff.

"What are you looking for?" Abigail asked hoarsely.

"Chisel marks and other signs of tampering."

Abigail left him to his work and strolled along the rest of the cliffside, determined to put some distance between herself and the spot of Fitz's death. She remembered having picnics along the cliffs as a child. The boys would climb along the rocks while she and Lizzy pretended they were brave travelers journeying across the ocean with the horizon in the distance. Of course, the ocean wasn't visible from the cliff, only towns far in the distance, but the wind blowing made it feel as if they were standing at the stern of a ship. The cliffs had always held a place in Abigail's memory as a pleasant reminder of her childhood, now those fond memories were permanently soured.

Carlyle stood from the ledge and rejoined Abigail.

"Did you find anything?" Abigail asked him, dreading the answer.

Carlyle shook his head. "If there was tampering, it's impossible to tell now. Someone could have taken a chisel and hammer to weaken that section of rock, however, they would have been taking a terrible chance in assuming Fitz or Merit would be the first to walk along that section."

"Is it possible that they were both being targeted?" Abigail asked.

"Perhaps. Either way, if someone was trying to murder one, then they had no qualms about taking the other out of the picture as well."

"True, but maybe the murderer wasn't taking as big of a chance as you think, Carlyle. Anyone who knows Merit and Fitz would know that Merit never walked that close to the edge of the cliff. He's always been wary of danger. Maybe being an orphan does that to a person. Fitz on the other hand was always taking risks."

"That is an interesting thought, Miss Abigail. Maybe you can bring one other question to light. Why choose that spot to attempt a murder? How would someone know young Fitz would walk along that section of the cliffside?"

"That's explained easy enough. As children, we often picnicked in that location. It's no surprise that Merit and Fitz walked along that section of the cliff."

"That means only one

of you would know of the significance of the spot," Carlyle said with concern.

"Not necessarily," Abigail told him. "Our parents all knew, Lizzy's aunt and uncle, and Fitz's brother, Eric. Eric used to join us when we were younger."

Carlyle considered the information.

"Do you think it could have been a murder?" Abigail asked.

"Perhaps the better question is what do you think, Miss Abigail? You knew Fitz Sawyer. You know your friends and your brother far better than I do."

Abigail shook her head. "I don't know. As Merit said, Fitz was difficult. He was loud and reckless and he always got on people's nerves. But I can't imagine anyone would want him dead."

"The question is motive, it's always motive. People lie and hide the truth which makes that question the most difficult to solve. It's impossible to tell if the ledge was damaged by nature or the hands of man. I believe we would be better off determining what happened to your brother. I suspect if we find that out, we will be one step closer to discovering what happened to Mr. Sawyer."

Abigail readily agreed to the plan. She was worried about Quincey, more worried than she had ever been before. What had become of him? Had he left willingly or forcefully? Was he involved in some way with Fitz's death?

"I suggest that we first question witnesses. Maybe someone will know something more about this situation. Who do you believe we should question, Miss Abigail?"

Abigail sighed heavily, disliking the answer to that question. "I suppose we better start with Fitz's parents, that is if they are around. You'll soon discover, Mr. Carlyle, just where Fitz learned his troublesome ways."

CHAPTER 6

If the cliffs had been unpleasant then Abigail was sure visiting the Sawyer estate would be torturous. She prepared herself for the conversation that may or may not take place.

"Mr. and Mrs. Sawyer spend most of their time traveling," Abigail warned Carlyle. "They may not even be home. However, given the war, I doubt they've been spending much time in Paris or Milan."

Abigail almost hoped that

Mr. and Mrs. Sawyer were gone. It would save her from an awkward and unpleasant topic of conversation. It was bad enough talking to them about pleasant topics. Discussing their son's death wouldn't go over well.

Abigail approached the mansion with growing trepidation. Although it was impressive, Sawyer House paled in comparison to Merit's home and even the Sinclair estate. It was as grand and expansive as the Sawyers could afford and they were always attempting to improve the place with a fortune they simply didn't possess. It had always been a stretch for them to build their home at Millionaire's Row and things had only grown worse after the Depression. Still, they traveled and threw their dwindling wealth at every impulse and desire.

She stopped at the door and turned to face Carlyle. "Um, maybe you should let me do the talking, Mr. Carlyle. I want to broach the topic carefully and I have some idea of how to get the Sawyers to talk with... civility."

Carlyle nodded his assent and gestured for Abigail to proceed.

Before she could change her mind, she knocked at the door.

No answer. Abigail breathed a sigh of relief. But before she could turn away, the door swung open.

Abigail recoiled, taking a step back. She had been expecting a servant or Mr. or Mrs. Sawyer but never would she have expected the man standing in the entry, a grim expression on his familiar face.

"Eric? You're home?"

Eric Sawyer leaned casually against the doorframe and studied her with dark, piercing eyes. "I could say the same about you, little runaway."

He was so different from

how Abigail had remembered him but in many ways, he was still the same. He was broader, especially in the shoulders. A mustache was on his face and his eyes were hard, more severe. The last time she had seen him was when he left home to join the military. He'd been called upon for training in the reserve right before she ran away. Abigail wasn't sure what to think about his being back but she knew it made her nervous and unsettled. She'd thought when he left that she would never have to see him again and she was perfectly satisfied with that notion. She didn't like that he was back, especially now, especially with Fitz gone.

"How long have you been back?" Abigail asked him.

"Since just before Fitz died," Eric answered, an unspoken challenge in his words.

Abigail stiffened and took another step away, placing more

distance between them.

"Are you still scared of me, *Abigail?*" Eric asked, purring her name, his voice snide.

Abigail squared her shoulders. "Are your parents home, Eric?"

"They're in Vermont. Who is this with you anyway?"

Abigail glanced over her shoulder and then swung her eyes back to Eric, wishing she hadn't taken her eyes off of him even for a moment. "This is my friend, Mr. Carlyle, a detective."

"A detective!" Eric exclaimed; a tinge of anger colored his tone. "Why is a detective here? This better not be about Fitz. That fool brought about his downfall, nothing to investigate about it."

"He's here to look into Quinn's disappearance," Abigail said shortly. "We need to talk to your parents."

"Question them you mean.

As I told you, they're not here and they weren't here when Quinn disappeared or when Fitz died if you suspect they're involved in any of that."

"Where were they then, when Fitz died?" Abigail pressed.

"New York," Eric said, his tone challenging. "They came back for the funeral when they heard what happened and then left soon after."

"And you were here when your brother died, Mr. Sawyer?" Carlyle asked.

Eric glared at him. "Yes, though I hope you're not implying anything by that. I completed my required year of service and was offered leave. Since they prefer to spend their time traveling, my parents have officially left the care of Sawyer House to me. I've returned home permanently. Little did I know, my brother would choose that moment to go traipsing recklessly on the cliffside and plunge to his death."

Abigail's mouth was dry. Her words lodged in her throat. She latched onto Carlyle's arm and without saying anything further to Eric, she dragged Carlyle away. She heard a snort of derision and then the door slammed shut and Eric disappeared back inside the house. Abigail pulled Carlyle forward, urging him on until the house was fading into the distance behind them.

"Miss Abigail, what's wrong?" Carlyle questioned.

Abigail still couldn't find her words. She shrugged and cleared her throat. Finally, she managed a vague response that she knew wouldn't satisfy her mentor. "I wasn't expecting Eric to be back."

"If there is something I should know that would be important to this case then I urge you to tell me, Abigail," Carlyle pressed.

"I'm just surprised, that's all." Abigail cleared her throat again. "Eric is difficult. He's always been difficult. He and Fitz never got along well. It's suspicious I suppose that he was home at the time of Fitz's death."

Abigail didn't tell Carlyle the rest. She didn't tell him how deep the hatred between the brothers had run. She thought of Eric's dark, stern eyes. Were they the eyes of a murderer? Abigail had no way of knowing.

CHAPTER 7

Abigail wished there were other places she could investigate, other people to question, anything to keep her out of that house a little longer. But nothing could last forever and she knew she had to be getting home. She dreaded the explanation she would have to give to her parents for why she had been gone all day. Abigail quietly opened the door to Stag Hall, hoping she might be able to slip in unnoticed but her mother was waiting for her in the entryway.

"Abigail, where were you?" Mrs. Sinclair hissed through gritted teeth.

"I was investigating the cliffs and talking to Merit."

Mrs. Sinclair's gaze spun to Carlyle who nodded in verification of Abigail's claim.

"You have no business investigating this," Mrs. Sinclair snapped at her daughter. "You should be in this house, safe, away from that awful cliffside."

"I'm only fulfilling my internship. My job is to follow Mr. Carlyle around, investigate crime scenes, and be available in the case of injury."

"I told you that you are to give up that internship at once. I asked Mr. Carlyle to come here so *he* could investigate, not you. When I couldn't find you today I… I thought you had disappeared like Quincey."

A cold feeling seeped into

Abigail's chest, a mixture of anger and pain. "You never seemed to care about my well-being before now!" Abigail snapped.

Mrs. Sinclair turned away. "I always wanted what was best for my children," she said coldly. "You're ungrateful, Abigail. You always have been."

Abigail wanted desperately to storm away but she didn't want to leave Carlyle. She had deserted him the previous night after finding out about Fitz's death, she wouldn't do so again. She reminded herself that she was no longer a child who could flee from trouble. She was grown, she had to stand and face the obstacles in her path.

She regretted her decision to stay when her mother announced that dinner was waiting. Abigail had always hated family dinners as a child. They never felt like family meals. Her parents insisted on eating at the banquet table, set up with the finest silverware and five-course meals. They sat with what felt like miles between them, with four forks and three knives, a triangular embroidered napkin, and a plethora of plates, bowls, and cups. Abigail still remembered what each utensil was for. It had been drilled into her mind so many times she was sure she'd be able to recite it even at her deathbed. Out of habit, Abigail took her usual seat at the table. She was almost shocked when she looked up and found Carlyle sitting across from her instead of Quincey. Her mother glared at her over the table, silently urging her to sit up straighter. Abigail took the opportunity to slouch even more. She even went so far as to rest her elbows on the table.

"Abigail, nice of you to *finally* join us," Mr. Sinclair told her coldly before he ignored her altogether and addressed only Carlyle.

Mr. Sinclair gave his usual dinner-time spiel. He talked of the Sinclair family legacy, his favorite topic and one Abigail had memorized almost as perfectly as her place setting.

"The Sinclair name has gone down in history as a family known for heroics and excellence," Mr. Sinclair began. "My grandfather was a hero who fought in the Battle of the Alamo. He had married a New Englander, my grandmother, and when he died she returned to Maine to her family. That's how the Sinclairs came up north."

"It's such a pleasant reminder of family history to have Miss Sutton around, she's a pure Southern Belle, sweet and simple," Mrs. Sinclair added. "Of course, my side of the family isn't from the south."

"Joan is from the Brightly family in New Hampshire, they come from old money, and their family dates back to the Revolutionary War," Mr. Sinclair explained.

Abigail rolled her eyes and resolutely focused on her food. She had always been of the opinion that it wasn't what your family did but what you did that left your legacy. She looked at Carlyle who was listening attentively. She was grateful for his diplomacy but she felt guilty for dragging him into this. Carlyle was reserved by nature and didn't care much for small talk. She knew it must be torture for him to sit through such a lengthy dissertation on the Sinclair family's pride.

The meal dragged on and on. Abigail fidgeted in her seat and noticed that Carlyle accepted not one but two cups of coffee after the food was taken away. Just when Abigail thought the meal had reached its end, her mother turned to her.

"Abigail, play the piano for us, like you did as a child."

"No," Abigail said firmly. "It's late. I'm going to bed."

"Abigail," Mr. Sinclair said in warning, "do as your mother says."

Abigail looked at her father. She saw the empty glass of wine in front of him. It had been refilled twice throughout the meal. She knew he wouldn't budge and she didn't want a full-blown argument, not in front of Carlyle. Trying to maintain her composure, Abigail rose from her chair and moved towards the piano in the adjoining parlor. The other dinner guests followed her into the room and took up seats to watch her play. Abigail stared at the piano with foreboding. She hadn't touched a piano since she'd left home. Her fingers hesitated over the keys.

"Play Fur Elise," her mother instructed.

Abigail's eyes widened. She looked at her mother with accusation. She saw that Mrs. Sinclair was set on the choice. Abigail swallowed hard and placed her fingers over the keys. Then she began to strenuously play. There was no sheet music so she had to strive to remember the complicated song as she played. Her fingers stumbled over the keys, making errors that rang violently loud in the otherwise quiet room. Sweat beaded on her forehead and her fingers cramped.

She heard her mother speak to Carlyle as she was playing, "She's terribly out of practice. It's a shame that Abigail didn't apply herself to her lessons more. Playing the piano, I believe, is the true mark of a lady. Abigail would have made a fine lady if she had put any effort into it."

Abigail missed a key and restrained the curse she wanted to exclaim in annoyance.

Much to Abigail's surprise, Carlyle rose to her defense. "Miss Abigail's skills are well suited to the medical field. She is very talented in that regard. It would be a shame for the medical world to lose such a prodigy in the field."

Abigail was pleased with the praise, especially at how uncomfortable it made her parents. As Abigail continued to labor through the lengthy song, her father rose and moved to the liquor cabinet.

"Care for a drink, Mr. Carlyle?"

"No, thank you, I don't drink."

"Oh, but remember that prohibition is over, Mr. Carlyle," Mr. Sinclair urged.

Abigail nearly scoffed. That had never stopped her father

before.

Carlyle shook his head. "Regardless, I don't drink."

Abigail struck the last key and let it ring out.

Carlyle clapped while her mother and father stayed silent.

Abigail headed to bed then, fully drained. She collapsed onto her bed, kicked off her shoes, and lay on top of the covers fully clothed. She hated this place and everyone in it. She just wanted to sleep but sleep evaded her. Try as she might, she couldn't stop thinking about the evening not to mention her earlier conversation with Merit. Seeing him so changed had startled her. She looked at her old writing desk and considered writing a letter to Arthur. She hadn't heard anything about the war since she had arrived home. Her father had never been one to care about what was going on outside of his haven. How was

Arthur? Every day that passed without news from him made her worry that something had happened. She wanted to write to him to tell him of her predicament. She missed talking to him. He had a practical mind and could always solve a problem rationally. But she couldn't think of the words to explain what was going on. She still didn't fully understand it herself. A letter would have to wait.

Abigail had a feeling sleep was pointless so she stood from her bed, determined to accomplish something. She would investigate Quinn's room. Maybe she would find something to explain why he had disappeared. She walked down the hall to the familiar room and pulled open the door. It was just as she had remembered it. The neatness, the books, the old movie poster he had snuck into the room without their mother noticing. It was so... Quincey. He had always tried to appease their parents and live up to their expectations but he was also unapologetically himself. Abigail closed the door behind her and went to sit on Quinn's bed.

"Where are you, Quincey?" Abigail asked aloud to the empty room.

Her eyes caught on something sitting on Quincey's bedside table. It wasn't one of his normal books. It was a small, leatherbound volume, a journal. Abigail reached for it, curious. She hadn't thought Quinn kept a journal and if he had then why hadn't he taken it with him? She flipped open the first page and to her surprise she saw in his handwriting her name scrawled on the paper:

> Abigail,
>
> If you're reading this, then Mother has somehow dragged you home because I've gone missing. I know you love a good puzzle so I've created this journal. If you can follow the clues and uncrack the code, you'll find me and learn why I left.
>
> Best of Luck,
> Quincey

A journal, filled with clues to find Quincey and learn why he left. Part of Abigail couldn't believe her brother for concocting such a plan and another part of her felt that it was so undeniably Quincey in every way. Part of Abigail wanted to place the journal back on the table and forget about it. She was afraid she might not like what answers she found at the end of the puzzle. Could this be Quinn's way of confessing to Fitz's murder? Abigail shook her head. She still couldn't find it in herself to suspect Quinn of murder even if all of the clues were pointing in that direction.

She quickly flipped through the entries of the journal and saw that they were stories. They were sloppy tales compared to what Merit might write but they were filled with a sense of whimsy that could only belong to Quinn. It made Abigail miss her brother more than ever. She had to find him. She grabbed the journal, determined to solve Quinn's puzzle even if it led to an answer that she didn't like. She prayed that she wouldn't regret her decision.

CHAPTER 8

The next morning, Abigail stayed in her room to read the first entry of Quinn's journal. She settled herself on her bed, weary from a night with little sleep. She laid the journal on her lap and opened to the second page.

Entry 1:
The story begins with five friends. The King, the Poet, the Jester, the Heart, and the Healer. They lived in a glass castle, a perfect kingdom where everything went their way. They spent their days romping

through the woods, careless of the pain of their subjects. One day they ventured deep into the trees, looking for a place to escape from the burdens of their expectant overseers. They discovered a hidden oasis where the stags came to drink, and reeds grew in abundance. There they lay for long hours on the edge of the lake, imagining themselves sunning on the banks of the river Lethe, gods of their lives, and heedless of everything but themselves.

The Jester was the first, as he always was, to grow bored of the carefree pastime. He decided he would take a swim in the oasis. He shed his fine coat and boots and effortlessly dove into the depths. The Poet was nervous and waited at the edge while the others went about their play. The Poet grew worried when the Jester was long in returning to the surface but the others berated him for his worry and ignored his warnings. But alas, the Jester was still delayed and the others began to notice his absence. They stood and approached the bank to peer into its murkiness and look for their companion.

"I think I see him," the Heart exclaimed, pressing a hand to her mouth in horror. "He's stuck in the weeds."

Indeed, the weeds twined around the ankles of the Jester like creeping snakes, holding him in the depths of the dark water. The King, the bravest of them all, jumped into the water without hesitation to rescue their friend. He dragged the Jester to the surface and flung him onto the banks. The Healer set to work, trying to revive him and finally, the Jester choked up the brine of the Lethe. The children returned home, having remembered that the pains of life are not so easy to forget. But they left behind something precious at the bottom of the lake. Innocence? No. Something more precious, an heirloom of the past. There lies the first clue, hidden in the silt and weeds. Remember.

Abigail closed the journal, feeling her heart thump with trepidation. She knew the lake that Quincey was referring to and she remembered well the day that the story described. But what lay at the bottom of the lake? What had been left behind? And why did Quincey choose that spot to leave his first clue? She felt a growing sense of unease as she wondered just what Quinn had in store for her with this little game of his.

Abigail knew she wouldn't find the answers she wanted until she went to the pond but she didn't plan to go alone. She dressed and met Carlyle downstairs. Her parents were gratefully still asleep and Carlyle had helped himself to some coffee and toast. Abigail joined him and set the journal on the table before him.

"What's this?" Carlyle asked.

"I couldn't sleep last night so I went to Quinn's room to look around. He left this, for me it seems. There are stories inside and clues to find him."

Carlyle opened the front page and read Quinn's brief note to her. "Interesting. I have a feeling I would get along well with your brother, Miss Abigail. This might be just what we need to determine what happened to him."

"I've already figured out where the first clue is. I... I don't want to go there alone."

Carlyle nodded and finished his coffee. "Then, we'll go together. Please, lead the way."

Abigail stepped outside into a bright, clear day. She was blinded for a moment. She wondered how a day could manage to be so beautiful when it felt like everything was falling apart in the world. She wondered if the soldiers fighting in the war felt the same whenever the sun streamed through the clouds as they fought and died for a country where men like her father continued life as if nothing were wrong.

Abigail led Carlyle through the trees, taking a path that led them out of reach of the stags grazing nearby. She tried not the think of where they were heading. Carlyle read through the short story in the journal as they walked.

"This *oasis* that your brother writes about, you think it's the pond?" Carlyle asked her.

"I know it is. I know the exact day that he's talking about. When we were young, we often swam in the pond but one day Fitz decided he wanted to dive down to the bottom. The rest of us were tired of his shenanigans for the day and let him do whatever he wanted without paying much attention to him. Only Merit was worried and stood watch. After a while, Merit warned us that he had been below the surface of the water for a long time. Merit was prone to worrying so we ignored him too. But a few moments passed and we realized that Fitz had been submerged for a long time. We all crept close to the edge to try to see what had happened. At first, Quinn thought that Fitz was playing a practical joke on us. It wouldn't have been the first time. But then Lizzy saw him tangled up in the weeds at the bottom of the pond. Quinn dived in to rescue him and I was able to get him to cough up the pond water when he reached the surface. Needless to say, we didn't swim much in the pond after that."

"Do you have any idea what the treasure left behind that Mr. Quincey mentions might be?" Carlyle asked.

"No," Abigail answered. "I

can't think of anything."

They reached the pond and Abigail sighed as she looked at it. It was murky and weeds and cattails surrounded it. The trees grew tall all around, offering a completely shadowed oasis in the forest. Small flickers of light filtered through the branches like fairies flitting around. Abigail remembered many hot afternoons spent around the earthen pool. It was funny really how so many good memories could be overpowered by a single bad one.

"Shall I jump in?" Carlyle asked.

Abigail was uncomfortably reminded of when Carlyle had jumped into a dangerous mire on their last case, offering no warning before he risked life and limb to uncover the truth. In some ways, Fitz had been like that but his recklessness was more for his own glory than to help others. Abigail remembered how terrified she had been when she'd realized Fitz was trapped at the bottom of the pond. She didn't want Carlyle to risk himself among the weeds. She knew she would have better luck in the situation. She knew the pond better than Carlyle did and she was a decent swimmer too.

"I appreciate the offer but I should do it," Abigail said.

"I hope you don't mind getting wet," Carlyle told her, just as he had before he'd jumped in the mire.

Abigail kicked off her shoes, removed her sweater, and then jumped into the water. The cold made her gasp and flail. She bobbed up and down a few times trying to stay afloat as the icy pinpricks of water overwhelmed her. Finally, the freezing cold turned into a bearable chill. Abigail managed to calm herself and after taking a deep breath, she dived down to the bottom of the pond.

Abigail groped blindly in the slightly murky water, kicking her feet to force her to greater depths. She forced her eyes open, the water burning. She dived deeper and deeper, her lungs burning with the effort of holding her breath. Finally, she reached the bottom of the pond. The weeds grew high and wild, more so even than when Fitz had gotten trapped. Abigail tilted so her upper body was towards the bottom of the pond with her legs floating above her to continue kicking against the water that threatened to pull her back to the surface. Abigail shoved her hands into the weeds, hoping there wasn't something with teeth hiding among the plants. She knew she was in approximately the same spot where Fitz had gotten stuck but she couldn't remember the exact location.

She refused to go back to the

surface until she found something. She felt slightly light-headed from holding her breath. Her fingers groped frantically between the weeds, looking for anything that might be the clue Quinn had left her. She feared she would have no choice but to surface but finally, her fingers brushed against something tangled in the weeds. Abigail yanked at it desperately. She felt something sharp slice into her finger. She nearly gasped and sucked in a mouthful of water with the quick, unexpected pain. Abigail shifted her grip, determined to rescue the object. She found a smooth surface without an edge and she held onto it. She pulled until the object was released from the weeds. She couldn't see what it was in the murk and she was starting to become desperate for breath. With a few urgent kicks, Abigail pushed herself back to the surface of the pond.

When Abigail surfaced, gasping for breath and trying to shove her sodden hair out of her eyes with her free hand, she opened her eyes and much to her surprise found that Carlyle was no longer alone on the bank of the lake.

"Merit?" Abigail asked, confused.

Merit's face broke into an expression of relief at her reappearance from the water.

"What were you thinking diving down there, Abigail?" Merit asked.

"Your friend was quite worried," Carlyle told her. "It was all I could do to prevent him from diving in after you."

"With what happened to Fitz down there I can't believe…" Merit shook his head.

Abigail looked up at him and blinked in confusion. "What are you doing here?" she asked.

Merit stared at her and she realized her current position, treading water, soaked and freezing, wasn't the best way to have a conversation. Merit seemed to realize it as well. He stooped and offered her a hand to help her out of the water. When Abigail reached for him, she remembered the object clasped in her left hand. Merit flinched away from the object and Abigail got her first real look at it. It was a small knife. Abigail placed it on the bank of the pond and reached again for Merit's hands. He helped her up and she sat panting on the grassy edge of the pool. She inspected her cut finger and was pleased to see that although the edge of the knife had pricked her, it was a superficial injury. She would clean it and bandage it later but she knew it was nothing to worry about.

"It seems your efforts paid off, Miss Abigail. I see you've found the clue," Carlyle said, picking up the knife and inspecting it.

"I remember it," Abigail said. "Quincey brought it here."

"I don't remember a knife," Merit remarked. "Did you really dive down there for *that*? Fitz almost died down there, Abigail. When I came to the pond and Mr. Carlyle told me you were diving, you have no idea how worried I was."

Carlyle shrugged out of his coat and handed it to a shivering Abigail. She accepted the gesture and felt a rush of welcome warmth as she wrapped herself in the coat.

"I found a journal, Merit. Quincey left clues behind to track him down. I don't know what to expect yet but the first clue led me here to retrieve that knife."

Merit shook his head in disbelief. "That sounds like Quincey. Please be careful, Abigail. Don't be as reckless as your brother."

"Why did you come down here, Mr. Raleigh?" Carlyle asked.

"I wanted to talk to Abigail about yesterday. I hope you know, Abigail, that I would never suspect Quinn of murder."

Abigail wrung out her hair and looked at Merit with understanding. "I know. I understand that the circumstances surrounding Quinn's disappearance are a little suspicious."

"It wasn't Quinn. I'm sure of it."

"Then, is there someone else you suspect, Mr. Raleigh?" Carlyle asked.

The light flashed through a gap in the trees and Merit suddenly looked terribly pale. He shook his head at Carlyle's words. "No. There's no one."

A thought occurred to Abigail. "Merit, how did you know I

would be at the pond?"

Merit was silent a moment as if he were considering how to respond to the question.

"I just felt like I needed to be here, I guess."

Merit's words made Abigail wonder if he even knew why he'd ventured down to the lake. He must have seen her and Carlyle but then why would he lie about that?

Merit looked into the depths of the pond as if trying to collect his thoughts. Suddenly he recoiled as if he had seen something. His mouth gaped in horror and he took a step towards the pond.

"What? What is it?" Abigail asked, frantically turning to stare into the pond to try to catch sight of what had scared Merit.

She couldn't find anything and when she turned back to face Merit he was shaking his head as if to clear it. He looked paler than before. He cleared his throat and offered Abigail and Carlyle an awkward nod then he turned and fled without another word. Abigail looked back at the pond. The surface was still and nothing but weeds were visible beneath the murky depths.

"What do you suppose that was about?" Abigail asked Carlyle.

The detective didn't have an answer.

Abigail reached for the knife and he handed it over. "This knife belonged to my great grandfather, Franklin Sinclair. He was the man my father was talking about last night who fought in the Alamo."

Abigail realized that her great-grandfather's initials were engraved on the handle of the knife and decorated with gold filigree. "As you would expect, this knife was a treasured family heirloom. One day Quinn took it from the house to show everyone. Fitz hadn't believed that the knife had been used during the Battle of the Alamo. In fact, according to my father at least, this knife was taken from my great-grandfather's corpse after the battle. When Fitz got stuck in the weeds that day, Quinn must have used the knife to cut him free and then dropped it as he helped Fitz to the surface of the pond."

Abigail studied the knife, trying to decipher what the clue attached to the object might be. She considered the initials **F. S.** and wondered if they held a deeper meaning. She would have to figure it out later. For now, she needed to get dry.

the journal to Carlyle to inspect. Abigail already had the strange words memorized:

> Abigail, _ _ I will _ _ nor _ _ _ _.
> My True _ was _. My _ _ was _ly, _
> _ a _ _. _ _ _ I _ that _ _ _ _ in the _
> I _ and I _ _. Then _ _ with _ _ and
> _ _. I _ to _. My _ _ _ that of a _. _ _
> _ _ _

"I couldn't figure out how to decipher it," Abigail told Carlyle.

Carlyle hummed in agreement as he studied the message, looking for its hidden meaning. "Your brother," he asked, "what does he do? What are his hobbies and talents?"

"You'd think he was a cryptologist or a spy if you based your knowledge of his off of that blasted journal, or worse a writer."

"He does have a talent for mystery."

"You'll be disappointed to hear of where he picked up that

talent. He used to buy dozens upon dozens of penny dreadfuls."

Carlyle cringed.

"Quincey's primary gift is a desire to learn. He was always eager to learn new skills. He and Fitz, much to all of our chagrin, learned how to pick locks on a whim. Quincey read about secret codes in some spy novel and decided he would invent his own. He tried to pick up writing techniques from Merit. He asked Lizzy to give him painting lessons. He even read through my medical books. He was much smarter than a lot of people gave him credit for. I fear that the path he was heading, he may have squandered those natural talents."

"It seems to me, Miss Abigail, that your brother still cultivated his talents. This is a difficult code; it will take time to crack it. If you insert the initials from the knife **F.S.** into the first blanks, it doesn't yield much. We won't be able to make progress on this riddle until we've solved the rest of Quincey's clues. Judging by the complexity of this puzzle, I think I will like your brother."

"Assuming he's not a murderer," Abigail said dryly.

Carlyle continued inspecting the journal while Abigail watched the sun reflecting off of the large glass windows of the ballroom. She could almost hear the music playing and the shuffle of feet striding the steps of a waltz. After a moment, she realized that she *did* hear footsteps, though not coming from the ballroom. Abigail spun around and saw a servant approaching across the lawn. She straightened and across from her Carlyle did the same.

After a moment, she recognized the uniform that the Sutton's servants wore. The servant caught sight of her and headed her way. The girl smiled at Abigail and handed her a small card.

"It's an invitation from Lizzy inviting us to tea," Abigail told Carlyle. Abigail turned to the girl. "Please tell Miss Sutton that we'll be there soon."

The girl scurried off with her news and Abigail stood from the wicker chair, brushing off her skirts. "Well, shall we, Mr. Carlyle? I for one need a break from Quincey's riddles and his terrible writing."

Carlyle followed her to Lizzy's house, a beautiful antebellum-style home with columns and a large wrap-around porch. Abigail felt like she had journeyed south every time she saw the mansion. Massive oak trees created a pathway to the house, with green lawns and a mossy fish pond to the side. The Sutton household was one of Abigail's favorite properties on Millionaire's Row, largely because despite its size and grandeur, it felt like a home. Abigail led the way to the porch and knocked on the large, white door. It wasn't a servant who greeted them but Lizzy's aunt, Georgia.

"Abigail!" Georgia exclaimed, pulling Abigail into an embrace. She smelled like orange blossoms, just as Abigail remembered her. "Oh, it's been much too long since we've seen you around here. And who is this?" She looked at Carlyle and held out her hand.

Carlyle took her hand gracefully. "I am Detective Carlyle. Mrs. Sutton, I presume? I've come to help investigate what happened to Mr. Quincey Sinclair."

"A terrible thing, truly. I'm so sorry about your brother, Abigail. I'm sure you'll find him soon," Mrs. Sutton said. "But please, come inside, Lizzy is waiting for you in the parlor."

Mrs. Sutton led them into the house and with a smile left them at the parlor where Lizzy stood and welcomed them.

"I'm so happy you came," Lizzy greeted. "Please, have a seat and I'll pour you some tea. We have biscuits too, and jam, and cream."

Abigail settled herself in a chair and gazed at the parlor. She remembered it from her childhood, though unlike most of the rest of the neighborhood, the Sutton property had changed in subtle ways. Georgia loved to decorate and as a result, the furniture was assembled in different locations, there were new paintings on the walls, the antiques were still on their shelves, the silver candelabras were still lined on the mantle, and the expensive China plates were still displayed hanging from the wall. The room still smelled the same, like honey and cinnamon. It was a relief to see the little changes without sacrificing her memory of the place. Even the event of taking tea in this room recalled events from her childhood. Ever since Lizzy had started visiting her aunt and uncle in the summer months, Abigail had joined her for tea at least once a week.

"I'm very interested in what you must do as a detective, Mr. Carlyle," Lizzy said, pouring him a cup of tea and leading the conversation as she always did. "I used to love detective stories as a child. I was raised on the best, Doyle, Christie, none of that nonsense that Quincey used to read. Is it true that detectives can see things about a person that no one else can?"

"Well," Carlyle answered, sipping his tea, "it is part of a detective's job to be perceptive. We notice things that others often overlook but it is far from a superhuman ability."

"Mr. Carlyle, won't you tell me something about myself that no one else would know, just like the detectives in the stories do?" Lizzy asked eagerly, leaning towards Carlyle with anticipation.

"Lizzy, don't be ridiculous," Abigail chided her friend. "Real detectives can't just magically know things about you."

"I admit, it's not my especial talent to read people," Carlyle told her. "I am far better at noticing clues that others overlook. But, if it would please you, Miss Sutton, I can try."

Lizzy clapped her hands and smiled. "Please do, Mr. Carlyle."

Carlyle set his tea aside and studied Lizzy so long and hard that she shrank back from the severity of his gaze, suddenly less eager to be examined. Abigail noticed that her eyes flitted away from Carlyle and latched onto a lace doily on the table.

Finally, Carlyle spoke. "I believe, Miss Sutton, that most people don't see you as you really are. Many see you as a selfless and empathetic girl who will always put others before herself. I see that you are indeed caring but you also know how to look out for yourself. You place yourself in situations where you will flourish. This house for example. I wonder why you came here when you have another home with parents who love you dearly. You prefer the north, I think, and you saw an opportunity for yourself among rich young suitors, your childhood friends. However, I also suspect that you've chosen wrong on more than one occasion and had to go to great lengths to right your situation. You're good at getting your way, Miss Sutton. Perhaps that is why you were so distraught when

Mr. Raleigh wouldn't let you in. However, you achieve your desires subtly. You don't like to exploit people to do so. And I see that you are the type who follows your heart above all else. You won't settle for anything short of what you desire most."

Carlyle finished his claim with a smile to show he meant no offense by his statement.

Lizzy was speechless. Abigail was as well. Abigail looked at her friend and wondered how Carlyle had detected so much. However, the words were far from unknown to others. Abigail had seen the same traits that Carlyle pointed out, though it had taken her years to understand Lizzy's character so well.

Lizzy raised a handkerchief to dap lightly at her lips. In a moment, she was composed again. A flawless Southern lady. "I admit that I'm not entirely sure whether to take your words as a compliment or an insult, Mr. Carlyle."

"I suggest you take them as neither, Miss Sutton. They are merely an observation."

Lizzy blinked and then she was fully herself once again. "Do Abigail next."

Abigail shook her head. "I would rather not have my deepest secrets read in such a way."

Carlyle grinned. "I can only guess what a person is like based on what I perceive but I can't be certain until they are tested through actions. Miss Abigail has already demonstrated her character through trial. She has proven the bravery and ingenuity that I originally suspected when I first met her."

Abigail cleared her throat to change the subject, uncomfortable at Lizzy's inquiring glare and certain that her friend would demand more information that Abigail was not comfortable sharing with her.

"Lizzy, please tell us everything that's been happening since I've been gone. I suspect I've only heard the beginnings."

"You'll probably want to hear about what happened between me and Fitz first," Lizzy guessed.

Abigail gestured for her to continue.

Lizzy sighed and looked intently into her cup of tea. "I had cared deeply about Fitz for some time," Lizzy began. "When I started to live with my aunt and uncle year-round, Fitz and I started spending a lot of time together. Quincey was different and Merit was working on a new poem or something, he spent hours locked away in his office and refused to talk to anyone. I realized that I not only cared for Fitz but loved him and he felt the same. Eventually,

Merit and Quincey reemerged from their respective isolations but still, Fitz and I were closer than ever before. One afternoon, Fitz found me alone. He pulled me aside and said 'Lizzy, I think you ought to marry me.' Well, it wasn't the type of proposal I would have expected but it was just like Fitz. I said yes and we agreed to a short engagement. Our families both approved and saw it as a good match. Quincey and Merit both had reservations but I suppose it's hard to accept change. I wanted to write to you about it all, Abigail, and so much else, but I didn't have an address to send any letters to."

Abigail smiled at Lizzy. "I'm sorry for everything that's happened, Lizzy. I know it must be hard for you most of all."

Lizzy's return smile looked fragile.

"Miss Sutton, what did Mr. Raleigh mean when he said that

Fitz treated you harshly?" Carlyle asked.

Lizzy sighed and took a long sip of tea before answering. "It was nothing really. Fitz just had a temper. It's something that runs in his family I'm afraid."

"That's no excuse if he hurt you, Lizzy," Abigail said. "Did he hurt you?"

Lizzy hesitated which was answer enough for Abigail. "It only happened once or twice," Lizzy finally said. "I know he meant nothing by it."

Abigail was about to say something more but Lizzy set down her tea, the cup rattling in its saucer.

"I know that you never liked Fitz, Abigail, and I can even understand why. Fitz was a difficult person to deal with at times. He was excessive in everything from his anger to his love. That's what I loved most about him. I *loved* him. But... I was considering breaking off the engagement."

Abigail hadn't been expecting such a confession. Neither had Carlyle. He sloshed a bit of tea on his shirt and hurriedly dabbed it away with a napkin.

"I didn't like Fitz's unpredictable tendencies," Lizzy admitted. "But then he died and I never got the chance to make up my mind and end the engagement. Maybe it's for the better. Fitz would have been devastated and so would have been our families and honestly I don't know if I could have gone through with it."

Abigail glared at her tea. Had Lizzy been planning to live with Fitz's abuse if he hadn't died? Would she have been willing to turn a blind eye to preserve appearance? In Lizzy's view, the issue was resolved and shouldn't be worried about any longer but it had taken Fitz's death to ensure it.

"Was there any awkwardness amongst your group because of your and Fitz's engagement?" Carlyle asked.

Lizzy laughed. "I think we all guessed that the engagement would happen at some point. My aunt always said I would end up with one of the boys it was only a question of which one. There was some awkwardness of course. Quinn was the one with objections and those didn't come until later when he caught Fitz raging at me. Quinn tried to talk me out of the engagement and when Fitz found out about it he didn't talk to Quinn for a week. It was the start of our problems. Fitz thought that Quinn was jealous. He thought Quinn loved me. I don't think he felt anything of the sort, at least nothing more than a childhood crush."

"What did Mr. Raleigh think

CHAPTER 10

"It seems that you've found yourself in the midst of quite a mystery, an incredibly unique one at that," Carlyle told Abigail as they walked back to the Sinclair estate.

"Surely you've seen mysteries like this one during your years as a detective, Mr. Carlyle," Abigail teased.

The conversation with Lizzy had unsettled her. She hated being back in the neighborhood, surrounded by the people she had tried so hard to avoid. She liked Lizzy, she really did, but she also knew that her old friend had grown up privileged and pampered. Abigail had left that life behind and she could never return to the way things had been.

"I think the most difficult part of this case isn't the death and disappearance but being back here."

"You're more than up for the challenge, Miss Abigail," Carlyle reassured her. "You've dealt with drownings and arson, murderers, and liars. You can overcome this challenge as you did the others. But I will offer you this one warning. Do not blindly trust those who you used to call friends. People change, I know that better than most."

"I know. They have changed, all of them, but in many ways, they're still the same. Maybe they've just become more themselves than ever. I find myself torn between love and disgust towards them. I have since before I left really. They live in their selfish worlds, only caring about themselves. Even Lizzy is like that to some extent. I believe what you said about her was right on the money, Mr. Carlyle. As a child, Lizzy was... precocious. She was the queen of our group from the moment she arrived in the neighborhood. The others, myself included, fawned over her. She was the star of our little circus and that was how she liked it. She always played the part of the southern lady but only if she got her way. I saw another side of her reveal itself on more than one occasion."

"I've found that people are complex beings, it is both a gift from God and a curse. People have the potential for both good and evil. What matters is what path they choose to take," Carlyle said.

"I truly believe that Lizzy cares deeply about others but

none so much as herself. Then there's Merit. He's always been absorbed in the world of his imagination, his poetry, and his quiet contemplations. Fitz was the most glaring example of self-centeredness. He was arrogant and reckless, and he never thought of how his actions would affect others. Quinn became much like Fitz over the years. His brilliance made him the undeniable leader of our group but he became equally uncaring for others. I admit that I was also stuck in my own world for a time. I loathed the prison that was my life. I lost myself in my textbooks and learning, striving for knowledge above all else. Eventually, I saw the true goodness that came from helping others and that's why I decided I had to escape my old life and do some good in the world. But as I started to realize the folly of our privileged positions, I felt only disgust towards my friends and their excess."

"You mentioned your friends but what was your relationship with Mr. Eric Sawyer, Fitz's brother?"

Abigail dreaded answering that question. She slowed her pace and with a hint of shame spoke, "I'm scared of him, Carlyle. I have been for a while now."

Carlyle looked like he wanted to ask more about the situation but seeing the look on Abigail's face he kept silent.

Abigail changed the subject. "I never really fit in with any of them. I think I was mostly included because of Quinn. I know well that I can't sink into the trap of thinking that the people I called my friends, the people I grew up with, are the same as they used to be. I've changed as well."

"I trust that you will handle the situation wisely, Miss Abigail. I only regret that this case has so personally affected you. I suggest you stay away from this matter with Fitz. I will look into Mr. Raleigh's concerns. They may amount to nothing after all. I can examine things from an impartial point of view and the others may unwittingly reveal something to me since I am an outsider as opposed to what they would be willing to discuss in your presence. Meanwhile, you can focus your attention on trying to solve Quincey's clues."

Abigail agreed, seeing the wisdom in Carlyle's suggestion. Besides, the reason she had returned in the first place was to find out what happened to Quinn. Maybe it was for the best that she stayed out of the investigation surrounding Fitz's supposed murder.

"Just let me know if there's anything I can do to help my friends," Abigail told him. That was all she could hope to do now.

CHAPTER 11

With Carlyle's warning ringing in her ears, Abigail set off to solve Quincey's next clue. Carlyle would follow his instincts and look into Fitz's death while Abigail worked alone to riddle through what her brother was trying to tell her. She glanced behind her at Carlyle's retreating back as he headed to Merit's home, intent on questioning the young man again, this time without Abigail or Lizzy present.

Abigail found a shady tree

to settle herself under away from the dangers of the wandering stags and opened the journal on her lap. She flipped past the first story to the next and shifted until she was comfortable.

Entry 2:
The Poet was a boy of few words and many thoughts. His mouth made no sound but his pen spoke for him. He could often be found in the treetops, notebook in his lap. The King and the Jester mocked the Poet for his ways, thinking him strange while, secretly, envy cowered in their chests. For the Heart and the Healer thought the Poet's words were charming things, though he rarely showed them. One day, the Poet wrote a sonnet specially crafted for the Heart. He refused to show any of the others but would have bestowed it upon her like a diamond ring. Jealousy

*raged in the Jester's chest at
the Poet's strive for the Heart's
preference. He conspired with
the king to bring about the Poet's
downfall and prevent the sonnet
from ever reaching the Heart's
delicate hands. They concocted a
plan and executed it to perfection.
They banded together and stole
the Poet's journal of words, then in
an act of malice, the Jester ripped
the pages from their binding and
tossed them to the wind. The Poet
was distraught and the Heart
was outraged at the injustice but
the Jester himself was filled with
remorse and apologized profusely.
The words were lost never to
be found again. But the sonnet
addressed to the Heart which
had been dropped in the midst of
the chaos was secreted away by
the hands of the King. He hid the
words somewhere where only he
could find them. At the beginning.
A man may 'die' but his words live*

on forever. In medias res.

As with the other story, Abigail easily recalled the day that Quincey wrote about. She remembered how Fitz and Quinn had stolen Merit's writing notebook and destroyed it. To Abigail, the act had always seemed cruel and unmotivated. She had never understood before why the boys would hurt Merit in such a way. He had been inconsolable, locking himself away for days before Quinn and Fitz finally apologized and begged him to come out of his room. There had been tension among the group for weeks after that and perhaps it was only Merit's desire to maintain his friends or their youthful tendency to forget disagreements quickly that preserved the relationship between the boys. Now that Abigail knew the real reason the notebook had been destroyed, she was disgusted at both Quincey and Fitz.

She was admittedly a little surprised to learn that Merit had written a poem for Lizzy but she quickly overcame her shock. Poems and stories were the only way Merit could truly express himself and they had all admired Lizzy. Lizzy had been particularly interested in Merit's writings and it was only a matter of time before he wrote something specifically for her. The question was, where would Abigail find the next clue, the missing poem?

Abigail read over the story again and then a third time. Her eyes kept catching on the last few lines. She thought back to the previous entry and the final word that had seemed so unimportant at first. 'Remember'. Looking back, the word took on a second meaning. Quincey wasn't just reminding her to remember the past, he was giving her another clue as to what she should be looking for.

"Remember the Alamo," Abigail murmured. "Remember."

The clue that Quincey wanted her to remember was her great-grandfather's knife, the same knife that had been used during the Battle of the Alamo. A spark of hope settled in Abigail's chest. Quinn knew that she wasn't as good at solving riddles as he was so he had left her additional clues to make her journey a little easier. He wanted her to solve the puzzle and find him.

Abigail surveyed the last line of entry #2. 'In Medias Res'. What was that supposed to mean? Abigail knew enough Latin from her studies to translate: 'In the Middle'. Still, the words held no meaning. She looked at the middle of the story for any additional clues but found nothing. The last clue had been concerning the object that Quinn had left for her. Abigail assumed this clue must have the same purpose. But how would she find the object? She didn't know where to begin her search. The poem could be hidden anywhere.

Another line of the story stuck out to Abigail. It might have been a throwaway statement but she was suddenly suspicious of every word that Quinn had inked.

"A man may die but his words live on forever," Abigail read aloud.

She considered for a moment why those words seemed so out of place to her when she realized that the word 'die' was emphasized in the writing. Why? She knew it was no mistake. It was a clue. Abigail turned her mind towards death. Her first thought was of the family graveyard, a small series of memorial tombstones her father had constructed in memory of the most renowned members of their family. There were no bodies in the graveyard, only reminders of the patriarchs of the Sinclair name. Abigail could think of no other place that better encapsulated the theme of death. She was certain it was where Quinn's clue was directing her.

She stood from under the tree and headed for the graveyard. As Abigail walked, she considered the other part of the clue, 'In the Middle'. Maybe it meant she should look in the middle of the graveyard. It was a small graveyard but Abigail took special care in inspecting each and every gravestone in the center of the gathering. There was nothing, not the slightest hint of disturbance, no poem, no clue. Frustrated, Abigail sunk down against one of the decorative stones. She was tempted to talk to the bust of the first of the

Sinclairs, the head of the family, Eisenhower "Ike" Aaron Sinclair. A man who, at least according to her father, had more than lived up to his impressive and lengthy name. Abigail missed Carlyle. He would no doubt find the truth in an instant.

"Maybe Quincey should have remembered that I'm not as clever as the rest of our ancestors," Abigail told the statue.

She stared at the names on the stone. Eisenhower "Ike" Aaron Sinclair, the founder of the Sinclair name. He would no doubt be disappointed in Abigail's lack of talent.

"At the beginning," she muttered to herself, remembering the line from Quinn's story. She sat up a little straighter. "At the beginning. In Medias Res."

She looked at the tombstone. Eisenhower "Ike" Aaron Sinclair. Ike Aaron, the middle two names. She knew it must be the clue Quinn had been trying to make her understand. Abigail could have hugged the lifeless bust of her great-great-great-grandfather with her excitement. Abigail made a mental note of the names, knowing it must be important to solving Quinn's puzzle but there was something else that she still had to find, Merit's poem. Abigail scoured the tombstone, looking from the top of the bust's head to the soil at the base of the stone. There was a slight crevasse in the stone and it was there that she found Merit's poem.

Abigail's eyes instinctively scanned the words but she quickly looked away. She felt a little like she was intruding on something private. She knew she shouldn't read something that Merit had written for Lizzy's eyes but she also knew that Quinn had already read the poem. Surely it wouldn't hurt to read it. It might be important to discover what Quincey was trying to tell her. She read the poem:

> *Never can beauty compare*
> *nor a good nature surpass*
> *Imperial; nowt impaired*
> *Eternal; our good compass*
>
> *Treading evil; good, trod towards*
> *When you made us realize*
> *painful lies sow new discord,*
> *life shifted to idealized*
>
> *Was your smile our lives reborn?*
> *Commenced to end all conflict*
> *mother's kindness; never shown scorn*
> *Fathers we had before, but strict*
>
> *Longed we always to escape*
> *life's ill pains; we sought your shape*

"Wow," Abigail murmured when she had finished.

She felt a suspicious flush

of heat in her cheeks when she had read the last word. Had Merit really written this for Lizzy? It was sweet and heartfelt which was no surprise from Merit but it was also incredibly personal. Abigail felt more than ever like she was intruding. A determination settled in her heart. She had to return the poem to Merit. She would make note of it in case it was needed to solve Quinn's puzzle but she couldn't hold on to something that Merit had spent a long time composing. The thought put into each of the words was obvious. Abigail felt more disgusted than ever at Quinn and Fitz for taking the poem. Merit should give it to Lizzy. He should have been able to give it to her long ago.

CHAPTER 12

With Merit's poem in her hand, Abigail trekked to her friend's estate to meet up with Carlyle and see if he had made any progress with Merit. Abigail held the poem like a precious heirloom. The paper was crinkled and the edges were frayed from the years but the words were still intact. She wondered what Merit would think when he saw the long-lost treasure again. Abigail reached the house and knocked. The servant from the day previous let her in with a sigh but no objection.

"Why did Merit, Mr. Raleigh I mean, release Mrs. Trenton from his service?" Abigail asked the new servant, still feeling unsettled by the idea of the pleasant woman who had practically raised Merit suddenly leaving.

The servant looked at her like she'd lost her mind. Abigail glared until he answered.

"I do not know for certain Miss, but the rumors are that Mr. Raleigh's attitude has become somewhat unpredictable. From my understanding, he dismissed Mrs. Trenton on a whim."

"A whim!" Abigail exclaimed.

The servant didn't stick around to answer any more questions. He gestured towards Merit's office. "You'll find the master in there."

The servant left Abigail standing alone in the entryway,

pondering over what she had learned. "A whim," she murmured to herself. "How strange."

Abigail approached the study and knocked casually on the door before softly easing it open. "It's me, Abigail," she announced as she let herself in.

She found Merit and Carlyle sitting across from each other in plush armchairs talking. Carlyle rose to his feet at Abigail's entrance. Abigail was a little startled at how pleased he seemed to be at seeing her. He looked strangely unsettled. Abigail brushed off the uneasy feeling Carlyle's behavior created. Whatever was bothering Carlyle, the expression was quickly masked and Abigail wondered if she had imagined the look on his face.

"Miss Abigail, I'm glad you are here. You should talk with your friend. It's been a long time since you've seen each other." Carlyle gestured her towards the chair he had vacated.

Abigail tried to question him with her eyes but he either didn't get the hint or ignored it. She was confused at Carlyle's strange behavior but she didn't say anything. Besides, she did need to talk to Merit. Abigail took a seat in the armchair across from him, feeling like she was swallowed up in the leather upholstery. Merit also looked very small in the oversized chair. He didn't look like the master of the house but like the same little boy she had known so many years ago.

"Are you making any progress with Quincey's journal?" Merit asked.

Abigail shrugged. "A little. It's led me to another clue."

Abigail handed Merit the slip of paper which contained the poem. "This is what the last entry of the journal led me to. I thought you should have it."

Merit took the paper but when he saw its contents and realized just what it was he was holding, he quickly shoved it back at her. "Take it! I don't want it."

Abigail held up her hands, refusing to accept the poem and wondering at Merit's frantic desire to be rid of it. "It's yours, Merit. You should give it to Lizzy like you always intended to."

"No, I can't do that. I won't do it." Merit looked into the distance as if lost in his thoughts, "I promise I would never..."

"Promised? Who did you make a promise to?" Abigail asked.

"Mr. Raleigh?" Carlyle asked with concern.

Merit wasn't looking at either of them anymore. His eyes were focused on something but Abigail couldn't determine what. She shifted in her seat, unsettled. Suddenly Merit snapped out of his trance and returned his attention to Abigail.

"You have to destroy the poem. Take it! I never want to see it again and Lizzy can never know about its existence."

Abigail took the poem, realizing that Merit would tear it up himself if she didn't. She didn't agree to destroy it though. She would hold onto it until the time was right. She was certain that Merit would eventually change his mind about the matter and regret his decision to have the poem destroyed.

"You should leave," Merit told them. "Please. Please leave."

Abigail stood, feeling unsteady on her feet. She wanted to ask Merit what was wrong and to apologize for upsetting him with the poem but she decided it was best to stay silent at least for the moment.

"Come, Miss Abigail, I

believe we've overstayed our welcome. We will see you again at your convenience, Mr. Raleigh," Carlyle said as he led Abigail out of the room.

Abigail felt her heart pounding as she followed after her mentor. Carlyle stayed quiet as they walked through the house and he didn't speak until they were well down the walkway outside.

"Miss Abigail, I beg you to answer my question truthfully, does Mr. Raleigh, Merit, have a history of psychosis?"

Abigail recoiled, appalled at the word. She didn't know how to respond. Finally, she found the capacity to form words. "Merit is a little strange, sure, but there's nothing *wrong* with him. Why would you ask such a thing? What exactly did you and Merit talk about?"

"I urge you not to worry too much but I had a very

strange conversation with your friend before you arrived," Carlyle explained. "I did not mean to startle or offend you with my question. It's only because that young man deeply intrigues me and I admit I'm a little worried about him."

"What are you talking about, Mr. Carlyle? Merit's just shaken up because of Fitz's death, that's all."

Carlyle shook his head. "I hope you're correct, Miss Abigail."

"You said you had a strange conversation with him. What happened?"

"I asked Mr. Raleigh to recount the events of the accident that took place on the cliffside. He seemed to struggle to recall the exact details of the event. I asked him to explain why he and Mr. Sawyer originally went to the cliffs. Young Merit couldn't remember. He only asserted that it was his idea and his fault. He began to explain what had happened several times but each time his words would trail off or he would stumble over what he was trying to say as if he didn't believe his own statements. He even outright refused to answer certain questions. He kept saying that he led Fitz Sawyer to the cliffs. He was insistent on that point. It was all very suspicious."

"Well, being interrogated by a detective can unnerve a person," Abigail defended her friend.

"If it were only that, it would be one thing. However, right before you came into the room, Mr. Raleigh froze as if in horror, cutting off the conversation altogether. He turned pale and stared at nothing then covered his ears and squeezed his eyes shut. Worried, I asked him what was wrong and he said that he couldn't stop hearing Fitz's scream as he fell."

Abigail shuddered at the words. She imagined Merit standing on the cliffside, unable to save his friend. "It's understandable that he's shaken up over everything. Merit lost his parents at a very young age, Carlyle. He came to rely almost exclusively on his friends. He's always been withdrawn, quiet, and anxious. This must be especially difficult for him."

"You say he relied much on his friends. Please, tell me what the friendship between you and the others was like, Miss Abigail," Carlyle requested.

"Well, Fitz and Quinn were partners in crime. Merit was always anxious and quiet but he kept close to the other boys and often kept them out of trouble. All three of them admired Lizzy and saw me as more of a nuisance I'm afraid. Merit was always the kindest to me."

Carlyle paused and glanced back at Merit's expansive estate. He eyed Abigail after a moment. She didn't like the look he gave her.

"I must ask you, Miss Abigail, to tell me everything. I know you haven't revealed all there was to your friendship with Merit. I will warn you that you shouldn't keep from suspecting him because of how you felt for him as a child."

Abigail blushed, reading between the lines of Carlyle's words. She couldn't deny the fact however and he was right. She needed to tell him everything. He was helping her on this most difficult case and she couldn't keep secrets.

"I'll admit that I may have had a slight affection for Merit as a child. I moved past that long ago but I do still care for him deeply as a friend. I'll try my best to avoid letting my feelings get in the way of finding out how Fitz died and why Quinn disappeared."

Carlyle nodded his approval. "There's one more thing that unsettled me about Mr. Raleigh's behavior."

"What is that?"

"You remember when he said something about a promise?"

"Yes."

"You asked him who he made a promise to but the way he spoke, his words were in the present tense, not the past. He said 'I promise' not 'I promised'. He wasn't making that promise to us and there was no one else in that room. So, who was he speaking to?"

A shiver ran down Abigail's spine as she considered Carlyle's words. The words mixed in her mind alongside what Carlyle had said earlier. 'Psychosis'. Abigail knew the word from her medical school studies. Brain chemistry wasn't her specialty but she knew enough about madness and insanity. She knew that couldn't be Merit, not the Merit she knew.

CHAPTER 13

Abigail hoped she wouldn't be home for long because she feared she would never get a good night's sleep in her childhood room. The memories were too potent and the furniture too small. She had a particularly fitful night filled with dreams or rather nightmares of her childhood with Fitz dressed in full Jester regalia, looming over her like a giant jack in the box. Lizzy had stood beside him with hearts painted on her cheeks and a lying smile on her face. Merit was curled into a small ball, clutching his head and muttering streams of incoherent words that floated in the air like the lines of a poem. And Quinn had been there too with his back perpetually turned, a crown of thorns on his head. Abigail woke early, desperate to push her dreams aside and solve the next clue.

Entry 3:
  The King and the Healer had
  deeper ties than the others,
  the unbreakable ties of blood.
  Though two people couldn't be
  more different, they were also
  alike in many superficial ways.
  The same nose, same eyes, same
  breathy laugh. They shared one
  other thing that was far from
  superficial, a distaste for their
  cruel overlords and a reliance
  on each other to survive the
  glass castle. The walls of their
  home were constructed carefully,

to do so. She knew it would hurt to return to that spot which had meant so much to her and her brother.

When Abigail found Carlyle waiting for her downstairs she told him, "I want to handle this next clue alone, Mr. Carlyle."

Carlyle readily agreed. "I understand. I was planning to spend the day questioning Eric Sawyer about his brother."

Abigail cringed. "Be careful. Eric has quite the temper."

Carlyle nodded. "You be careful as well, Miss Abigail. The past can be a dangerous thing."

Carlyle beat her to the door and as Abigail was preparing to follow after him, her father appeared silhouetted in the doorway, blocking her path. Abigail was surprised. Her father wasn't usually awake so early. She saw the dark circles under his eyes and wondered if he'd been up all night. Surely, he hadn't been waiting for her. Then again, she had been trying her best to avoid him at all costs.

"A word, Abigail," Mr. Sinclair said.

Abigail looked for a way to escape but could see nothing to help her. She slowly approached her father. He led her into his office, a room that she had always dreaded. She'd been warned time and again as a child to not wander into the room and whenever she *had* been brought inside it was always to receive a punishment of some kind. Abigail stood in front of his desk like she was a child again with her hands clasped behind her back and her spine straight. Her father stared at her long and hard. Abigail waited for him to speak, knowing he would expect her to be silent until spoken to.

"I expect you will return home permanently now," he finally

said.

A spark of rebellion surged in Abigail's chest. "I see no reason why I would do that."

"You've already been an embarrassment to this family in thinking you could run off to be a doctor of all things. It's time to put away such nonsense."

"It's not nonsense. I know I can be a doctor. It's been difficult and I still have a long journey ahead but I know that I'm capable of it. Maybe I got that reckless perseverance from you, Father."

Mr. Sinclair shook his head. "You will change your mind soon enough. Let's just hope you don't wait until it's too late. If you keep treading your current path then you won't always be welcome to return."

Abigail put her hand on her father's desk and leaned towards him. "That is precisely why I have no desire to come back. What kind of father would tell me I'm not welcome to return home?"

Mr. Sinclair glared at her. "What kind of daughter would leave, embarrassing her family in the process?"

"Well," Abigail said, pushing away from his desk and towards the door, "I guess we're both a disappointment then. I suppose there's no mending that."

Abigail strode from the room, head held high but beyond her father's sight, tears were gleaming in her eyes.

Abigail headed for the tree, her and Quincey's tree. It was on the edge of the property, hidden in a place where their parents would never venture. Abigail found it easily and with it, she found the memories that were attached to the place. She remembered with a pang in her chest how close she and Quinn used to be. When they were very young, they had been inseparable, two sides to the same coin. Then, they had pulled apart until the connection between them finally snapped. Abigail wished things had been different but she also saw that it was inevitable given the paths they had taken in life.

Abigail approached the tree and stepped inside. It was a tight fit now that she had grown but the concave center of the truck still allowed her entry. She stood there for a moment, hand brushing against the rough bark as the memories surrounded her. There were a few remnants of Quinn left behind. Abigail saw the signs of the preparations he had made, thinking they would run away someday and leave everything behind. There was an old canteen, a kitchen knife, and a compass. 'Navigate the past, read the needle.' Abigail reached for the compass but then, remembering the words of the riddle, she instead peered closer to read the needle's direction from its position on the ground.

"North, Northeast," She muttered.

Satisfied that she had read the direction correctly, Abigail reached for the compass. Maybe it was important in another way for solving the riddle and she didn't want to return to the tree again if she could help it. With the compass in hand, Abigail went to find Carlyle, her heart heavy with memories as she went.

CHAPTER 14

Abigail could hear the shouting from the driveway. When she heard the undeniable tenor of raised voices, she broke into a run approaching the Sawyer estate. As she drew closer, she recognized Eric Sawyer's tone. She hoped that Carlyle wasn't in trouble. When she reached the door of the house she found that her mentor had found himself in somewhat of a pickle. Abigail had caught up to him just as he was being thrown out of the Sawyer estate.

When Eric caught sight of Abigail approaching he turned his sour face on her, insulting her. "You filthy, lying wretch! How dare you spread such lies and stick your feral detective on me!"

Abigail took a step back at the insult but before she could respond, Eric turned his animosity on Carlyle again.

"As for you, *sir*, I fear for the great population of Chicago with someone as foul as you walking their streets! If I never see your face again, it will be much too soon."

The door was slammed shut before Abigail could say a word. She turned to Carlyle with wide eyes.

"What just happened?"

Carlyle turned away, looking slightly sheepish. "I may have unintentionally revealed to Mr. Eric Sawyer that he was a suspect in the case of his brother's death."

Abigail winced, knowing

Eric's temper and how he would react to such an accusation.

"I did warn you to be careful, didn't I?" Abigail said. "I am interested though, did you learn anything important before you were thrown out?"

"I learned that Mr. Eric Sawyer was at home at the time of Fitz's death, however, there is no one to verify that claim. The Sawyer brothers fought nearly constantly upon Eric's arrival home. According to Mr. Eric Sawyer, they couldn't say two civil words to each other and the fights frequently escalated into physical brawls. On the day of Fitz's death, there was a particularly nasty disagreement. Eric had been trying to throw Fitz out of the house permanently. Fitz mocked Eric saying he was far from the war hero he claimed to be since he had spent only one year in the service before leaving as soon as possible.

I also discovered empty alcohol bottles scattered around the house. I suspect both brothers had been drinking excessively."

"That's no surprise," Abigail commented.

"Eric informed me that Fitz completely lost his mind when Eric threatened to kick him out of the house. According to Eric, Fitz went after him with a knife. I believe a broken bottle I found lying in the corner of the room is the more likely culprit."

"Eric was always prone to exaggerate," Abigail said.

"Indeed. Though there is evidence that Fitz did attack his brother. Eric showed me a jagged wound on his forearm made by the weapon. The wound was significant and clearly, the assailant meant to do damage."

"I imagine it was after this ugly fight that Fitz went with Merit to walk along the cliffs?" Abigail asked.

Carlyle nodded. "I asked Eric if he went after his brother to finish the fight. Eric responded that he wanted to. In his exact words, 'I wanted to show that punk a lesson'. But he claimed he didn't go through with his plan. He said that he controlled his anger and stayed at the estate."

Abigail scoffed. "I find that hard to believe. He was never one to control his anger before."

"I agree that the claim could have easily been a lie, especially given the behavior he's demonstrated. He had a reason to be angry with his brother and while he may not have wanted his brother dead, a simple shove on a cliffside would be enough to send someone over the edge accidentally."

"If that were the case then it means Merit is covering for Eric. But that doesn't make any sense,"

Abigail commented. "Unless..."

Carlyle gestured for her to continue.

"Do you think Fitz could have wandered out of Merit's sight at any point during their walk?"

"It's possible, though I wouldn't discount the idea that Merit Raleigh may not be the most reliable witness in the first place."

"You think he's lying?"

"Maybe he is lying to himself."

CHAPTER 15

Abigail set to work, reading the next journal entry and trying to solve Quincey's next puzzle. She was eager to put the confrontation with Eric Sawyer out of her mind and the journal was the perfect distraction. Abigail flipped open the leatherbound book and read.

Entry 4:
Winter came to the glass castle and with it the departure of the Heart. It was a trying time for the friends. The separation of so many months seemed to last for

longer periods each year. However, the King's father never allowed boredom to flourish in the kingdom. There was plenty of entertainment for those left behind. The Dionysian madness fell on the kingdom. Extravagant celebrations were thrown every night. The Jester's father joined in gallantly and the Jester was often found at the King's estate along with his elder brother. Music roared through the endless halls and the Healer was often called upon to conduct striking performances for onlookers, fingers moving fluidly over the pianoforte. She was ceaselessly rebuked by the Queen mother for any imperfections. The King and Jester went about their plans. They spoke of the future and how much they detested it. When the Healer was finally able to escape her constraints, she would join them. She warned them of the path they were taking, a dangerous route that would lead them to destruction. The boys despised her warnings and considered them judgmental. But they should have heeded her words. One night, the Jester displayed a prized possession to his companions. It was his family ring which rightfully belonged to his elder brother. The Jester had stolen it right after his father bestowed it to his brother. He secreted the ring away to the King's estate and while a party roared with life in the background, he showed the treasure to the King and the Healer. The Healer berated him for stealing something so important that was not rightfully his. But the Jester mocked her again, fiercely, for her words. He claimed that she was always judging him for being less than perfect. He spoke terrible words to her that night and claimed that she wasn't really one of them, they were only required to include her in their schemes because of her ties to the King. The King, coward as he was, didn't defend the Healer. Hurt by the words, the Healer left the King and the Jester to their path of destruction. If only they had listened to her words of wisdom and followed her advice because that night tragedy struck. The boys snuck into the ballroom and thieved quantities of the illicit liquid mirth that fueled the party's extravagancies. Their minds grew foggy and their actions senseless and in that state of intoxication, the Jester lost the ring. Despite their efforts to search the entirety of the glass castle, the Jester and the King could not locate the ring. And so, when its presence was missed, the Jester was faced with a decision. The Jester's brother knew he had taken the ring. He claimed that he would forgive if the treasure was restored to its rightful owner. But the Jester no longer had the ring. His hubris rose to the surface and instead of revealing the fact that the ring was lost, he lied. He told his father and brother that he had stolen the ring and hidden it where no one would ever find it. He refused to give up its location no matter what they did to him. And they did much to him that night and the nights following. They beat him in turns until he could scarcely keep his feet. They locked him in his room as if it were a prison. They kept all visitors away from him and rationed him to two bland meals a day. Still, he did not cave. He couldn't. Eventually, the Jester was released from his confinement but what he had done was never forgotten. His brother hated him from that day forth with a passion. He never spoke another word to the Jester nor gave him so much as a glance. The father of the Jester was likewise cold but he had always been that way so it was not as cruel a blow. But, years later, when it was much too late, the day the Jester's body was discovered at the base of a cliff, the King in a similarly drunken state to that night stumbled and fell. His eyes lit upon the dull gleam of old metal. He had discovered the ring. It was hidden in a crevice. Can you guess where it was? The King left the ring in its hiding place for you to find. It lies at the junction between stories.

The story made Abigail distinctly uncomfortable. She was starting to become annoyed at Quinn for making her relive the most disturbing of her childhood memories. She recalled the night in the story as one of horror. She had wanted to hide from those she thought were her friends and family. It was one of the occasions when Abigail had known beyond any shadow of a doubt that she didn't belong. She hoped she could solve the journal quickly so she could put the past behind her and never open that chapter of her life again.

Abigail began to look for the 'junction between stories.' She knew at least that it was somewhere in the Sinclair Estate. Stag Hall was where Fitz had lost his family ring and Abigail knew that was the clue that Quinn wanted her to find. She felt pained at the idea of him discovering the ring the day that Fitz died, too little too late. That ring had caused so much pain and turmoil and to find it after Fitz's death would only add to the pain associated with it.

As Abigail searched the house, she was grateful to avoid

her parents as she worked. Her father had gone into town to his club to meet with some friends and her mother was having tea with Georgia Sutton. Carlyle, spirit dampened after his conversation with Eric Sawyer, had taken to investigating Quinn's room instead of speaking to any other witnesses.

Abigail started her search in the library, perusing the gaps between every bookshelf. She had no idea what a juncture between stories meant but she suspected it had something to do with books. She pulled books from the shelves, looking in the gaps between spines. At one point she suspected Quinn had hollowed the inside of a book out and hidden the ring there, like an ally sneaking a weapon into a prison to help a prisoner escape. She looked at suspicious titles, 'The Ladies Guide to a Good Marriage', 'Ring Around the Rosie: A History of Plagues and Pestilence', and a particularly terrible mystery story that Abigail thought would be just up Quinn's alley, 'The Ring of the Pharoah'. None of the books were tampered with.

Abigail moved on to her father's office to inspect the books there and still found no luck. So, maybe it didn't have to do with books. Stories could be shared in other forms. Abigail found the hall of family portraits. Maybe the story that Quinn was referring to was more personal, the story of their family. A juncture could be referring to the gap between generations. Abigail checked behind each portrait and still found nothing. She felt a wave of frustration wash over her. Why had Quinn made the clues so hard to follow? Abigail was no detective. Fortunately, she did have one handy.

She went up to Quinn's room to find Carlyle.

"I need your help," she told him. "Quinn mentioned a juncture between stories in his journal. I'm supposed to be looking for a family ring. I've checked the library, my father's office, and even the hall of portraits but I can't find anything."

Carlyle took the journal, carefully read the entry, and then read it again. The furrow of confusion between his brows did little to comfort Abigail. She took a seat on Quinn's bed and waited for Carlyle's response. Finally, he closed the journal and handed it back to Abigail.

"I'm afraid you've already searched in the areas I would suspect. I'm just as confused as you. But I can help you look again. Maybe, if we walk through the house, we can find something that makes sense."

Abigail sighed, annoyed at the lack of a solution but she saw no better course of action to take so she stood and followed Carlyle out of the room. They went around the same path Abigail had taken before. They checked the library, the study, the parlor, and the hall of portraits. They even read through old cookbooks in the hopes of discovering something. Finally, they returned to the entryway, having searched every nook, cranny, and crevasse they could think of with no success. Defeated, Abigail sank to sit on the bottom step of the stairs leading to the second floor.

"This is pointless. How are we supposed to find a 'juncture between stories?'" Abigail complained.

Carlyle stood pondering for a moment before his face suddenly lit up. "That's it!" he exclaimed.

Abigail looked up, studying her mentor with fragile hope.

"Don't you see, Miss Abigail? The juncture between stories isn't books or paintings. You've found it without even realizing it."

"I don't understand."

"The juncture between stories is the stairs that connect the two stories of the house."

The moment Carlyle spoke the words Abigail knew them to be true. She stood from the stairs, amazed that she hadn't seen it before. Of course! Abigail hurriedly set to work searching the staircase for clues. It didn't take her long to find a cracked corner on the bottom step and when she wiggled her finger into the hole, she brushed something cold and metallic. Abigail pulled out the ring and with it a tiny scrap of paper. In Quinn's handwriting, two simple words were scrawled on the paper: *Dangerous Future*.

Abigail, holding the ring in her hand, suddenly felt defensive of Fitz in a way she never had before. She felt incredibly, unexplainably, sorry for him. She felt his absence keenly, like a rotting recess in her chest. Bitter tears sprang to her eyes that she fought back. She sunk back onto the stairs, clutching the ring close and remembering Fitz.

"Fitz took this ring from his brother the day it was given to Eric. He wanted to show it to me and Quinn and get Eric in trouble for letting it out of his sight. It was their family ring and Fitz lost it in his carelessness," Abigail explained to Carlyle. "He was too proud to admit his fault and said he hid it. He refused to reveal the location of the ring because he didn't know where it was but his father and brother thought he was lying. They beat him terribly for his perceived rebellion. Then they locked him in his room with two meals a day for a week. They wouldn't let anyone in to see him. When Fitz finally came out of that prison, he was bitter, bruised, and defeated. His father was cold as ice towards him from that point on but Eric was so angry he refused to so much as acknowledge Fitz's presence for months. After that, every word between the brothers led to a fight. That's why I became afraid of Eric. I still can't believe that so much trouble, so much bitterness, and hatred, could happen all because of this little, insignificant ring."

Abigail's throat tightened as she thought of the terrible place she had been raised. She despaired at the wickedness she and her friends had experienced and how her friends had started to morph into the same monsters that had tormented them throughout their childhood.

Maybe solving this case was pointless. Fitz was already dead. There was no saving him. Solving the mystery wouldn't bring him back. Abigail was afraid to find

Quincey and see what kind of person he had become. If he had murdered Fitz then she never wanted to know the truth. Abigail wanted to remember her brother as he had been when they were children.

"I don't know if I can do this anymore, Carlyle," Abigail confessed. "I'm sorry for dragging you into the mess."

Carlyle sat beside her on the stairs. "Miss Abigail, you helped me in more ways than one in our previous case. I intend to return the favor. My job is to help people and I see a great need for help here. I want to help you solve this case but I've also discovered that I want to help your friends. I urge you to persevere. I feel that the answers to this mystery are close at hand."

"I just wish I had run far enough away that no one would have found me."

Carlyle patted her shoulder

sympathetically. "I recognize an evil in this place and I understand why you left. I am glad for your sake that you did. But I trust that God has a reason for your return just as He had a reason for your departure. You have the chance to help your old friends. It may be too late for Fitz Sawyer but I can see great hurt in Merit Raleigh and Elizabeth Sutton. You may be the only person who can heal that hurt, Abigail."

"Maybe Quinn left because he knew it was the only way to make me come back," Abigail said laughingly. "He always loved a good game. I miss him."

"You will see your brother again, Miss Abigail, and when you do, I am confident you will make amends."

CHAPTER 16

Abigail retreated to her room early that night, worn from the adventures and trials of the day and eager to find an escape. She closed the door behind her, determined to not open it for anything short of a fire or an earthquake. Once she was certain she wouldn't be bothered, Abigail took a seat at her desk and pulled out a paper and pen. She settled herself into her seat and began to write.

Dear Arthur,

I hope and pray that you are well. It's been so long since I've written to you. You'll never believe where I've found myself and you would hardly know what to think. I've kept this secret even from you, dear friend. You know so little about my past and that has been by design I'm afraid. I wish I had trusted you with everything before but I was a coward and I didn't want you to think differently of me. Someday I will reveal it all to you. For now, only know that I have returned to my childhood home. My brother Quincey has gone missing and I intend to find him. But there is more than that to keep me busy. A childhood friend, Fitz Sawyer, is dead and while some suspect it was an accident, others are worried it was murder. My mentor, Carlyle, and I have come to find the truth. I find it strange

and unnerving to be back here. The friends I knew from childhood have become nothing more than distant memories. I've discovered that it is my new friends whom I've come to rely on more than anyone, you especially, Arthur. You know that I'm not much for prayer but I pray every night for your safe return from the war.
Yours truly,
Abigail

As she signed off on the letter, Abigail set her writing aside and considered Quinn. She'd thought writing to Arthur would make her feel better, instead, her mind just turned more sharply towards her brother. Would she ever see Quinn again? And if she did see him, then what would she say? She couldn't do this anymore. Nothing that had brought her comfort and peace in the past seemed to have any effect. Her old life weighed on her. She didn't have her family to turn to or her friends. She felt so alone, to the point of despair. Everything was going wrong. Quincey was gone. Fitz was dead. Merit was different and Lizzy was frustratingly the same. Abigail felt like there was nothing she could do. All her life she had tried to fix everything but this was something she simply could not fix. She needed help. In her desperation, her eyes fell on the Bible that Carlyle had given her and she began to read it. She felt a sense of peace as her eyes scanned the words. Maybe, just maybe, she wasn't as alone as she thought.

CHAPTER 17

Abigail rose late the next morning, her mind a mess of confused emotions. When she opened her eyes and saw the brightness filtering through her window, she felt that she had lost essential hours in the search for her brother. She wasn't sure why but there was a nagging in her chest that warned her time was limited. She set to work right away on Quincey's next clue.

Entry 5:
Years passed in the kingdom and

the glass began to fracture. Fissures spread until the façade was destroyed. The King, the Jester, and the Poet were sent away to be disciplined and transformed into the perfect pawns of the kingdom. But their schooling came at the cost of their morals. The Poet's frailty rose to the surface. The King and the Jester watched as their companion's mind changed and the innocent boy they knew became somewhat erratic. The Poet began to rely on his friends more than ever but they were quite simply, unreliable. The Jester began to conduct elaborate and dangerous pranks on the schoolmasters and his fellow pupils. He put himself in the place of chief danger, scaling walls, placing pins, and sneaking out past curfew. The King followed along, for once a loyal subject, eager to see the danger and intrigue he and his friend could cause while the Poet looked on in dismay and worry. By some terrible twist of fate, the boys were never caught nor disciplined. They became even bolder and believed they were invincible. Maybe they were. But not everyone was. It was inevitable that one of their pranks would go too far. The Jester thought it would be great fun to lock one of the students outside the dorms in the middle of winter. The student was found in the morning, nearly dead from exposure, and was sent home immediately. The Jester laughed off the occurrence, saying it was nothing to worry about since the student didn't die. But the Poet was distraught over the prank gone wrong and the King started to feel remorse of his own. That remorse clung to him like a foul odor and made him bitter. He began to feel less at ease around the Jester. But things didn't come to a head until the boys returned home, their educations complete. The King found the kingdom in shambles when he returned. The Healer was a shell of her former self, overcome by the weight of the Queen Mother's impossible expectations and with the King's father seeking an alliance between her and another kingdom to send her away. The Healer expected sympathy and aid from the King when he returned but she found none. He had become cruel and unjust, especially as his morality fought within himself. It wasn't long after that she fled the kingdom. He hadn't even realized the moment when she was saying goodbye. She didn't say it in those specific words. She only said, "I've changed, so have you, I hope that one day our paths will be going in the same direction again, but for now I have to go my own way." She handed him a letter and told him to wait to read it. That night, when he realized she was truly gone, he opened the letter. Then the King felt true pain and regret. He saw his mistake, the monster he'd become. He fought against his confusion and regret for a long time, being pushed away from and pulled towards the ill example of the Jester during the process. At last, he found a secret that he never would have expected. A revealing of his sinful heart and fallen nature. He turned his path and he kept the letter, hidden in his only place of refuge, the only place that was solely his, as a constant reminder of how much he had to change to make amends. Words hold power. Seek the words, find the truth.

The letter. Abigail's heart wrenched inside her chest. She remembered it well though she couldn't remember the exact words written inside. She'd been angry and hurt when she'd written it. She'd never thought it would get through to Quinn. She'd half expected him to destroy it instead of opening it. She had to find it.

Abigail had a suspicion she knew what room Quinn considered his only place of refuge and the only place that was entirely his. She followed the riddle to Quinn's room. She didn't seek Carlyle before she entered. She wanted to solve the riddles alone if she could. She still didn't want to share such a sensitive side of her past with him.

Abigail began to search her brother's room. It was impossible to not think about his well-being as she sifted through his belongings. Everything reminded her too much of Quincey. She missed him more than she ever thought she could.

Finally, Abigail pulled open a drawer of his dresser and it was there that she found the letter. Abigail knew that Carlyle had searched the room before. She knew he must have seen the letter. He would have opened it and read it to make sure it wasn't something important like a confession. But even with its obvious relevance to the case of Quincey's disappearance, he'd left it there for her. Abigail clutched the letter to her chest and went to sit on Quinn's bed.

Tears came to her eyes as she remembered how she'd felt when she'd written the letter. She had felt betrayed to her core. Quinn had changed and Abigail had seen both during his absence and upon his return that she no longer belonged in her home. She was an outcast among those who should have loved her and cared for her. She had thought things would get better when Quincey returned but, when they only got worse, she knew she had to run away.

Abigail pulled the letter out of its envelope and saw that the page was crinkled as if it had been read many times. There was the sign of water damage in the corner, a teardrop perhaps. And at the bottom of the page, written in Quinn's handwriting were two words, the next clue, 'My Remorse.'

Abigail read the letter:

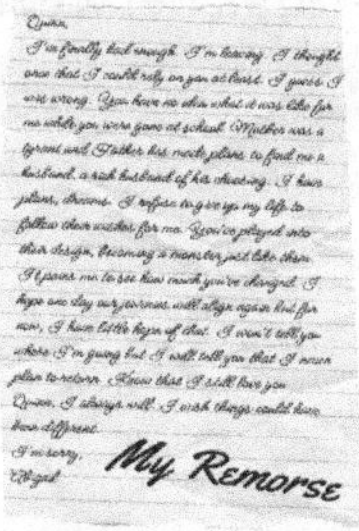

Quinn,

I've finally had enough. I'm leaving. I thought once that I could rely on you at least. I guess I was wrong. You have no idea what it was like for me while you were gone at school. Mother was a tyrant and Father has made plans to find me a husband, a rich husband of his choosing. I have plans, dreams. I refuse to give up my life to follow their wishes for me. You've played into their design, becoming a monster just like them. It pains me to see how much you've changed. I hope one day our journeys will align again but for now, I have little hope of that. I won't tell you where I'm going but I will tell you that I never plan to return. Know that I still love you Quinn. I always will. I wish things could have been different.

I'm sorry,

Abigail

My Remorse

As Abigail read the words she had written to her brother, she regretted the necessity of them. However harsh her letter had been, she at least knew it had affected Quinn, perhaps even enough to make him change.

Downstairs, the unmistakable sound of the doorbell ringing floated up to Abigail's hearing. Distracted by the letter, she vaguely listened as the door was answered and she could hear Carlyle's voice speaking to whoever was calling. Abigail carefully folded up the letter and placed it back in Quinn's drawer. She would find her brother. She had to. And when she did, she would fix things between them.

CHAPTER 18

Abigail couldn't help feeling numb to the world around her as she thought about the letter and her brother. 'My Remorse,' he had written at the bottom of the page. She had a feeling those two words were more than just a clue. Did Quinn feel remorseful because of what had happened between them? Abigail considered that question as she descended the stairs to see who was speaking to Carlyle at the door.

As she approached, Abigail

heard raised, frantic voices. She picked up her pace and turned the corner to find Lizzy standing in the doorway. Abigail knew immediately that something was very wrong. Tears streamed down Lizzy's face. Her cheeks were flushed from exertion and worry as if she had run to reach them.

Carlyle spoke authoritatively, trying to calm and console the frantic girl. "It will be alright, Miss Sutton. Please, tell me what's wrong."

"Lizzy?" Abigail asked, approaching.

At Abigail's appearance, Lizzy let out a sob. Abigail pulled her friend into an embrace and let Lizzy shake and cry in her arms until she was able to pull herself together enough to speak.

"What's wrong?" Abigail pressed. "Did something happen?"

Lizzy pulled away and wiped at her eyes. "It's just that

I was with Merit and I'm terribly worried, Abigail. I came to his house this morning and I tried to talk to him but he had locked himself in his room. I thought he was past pushing me away. He said he couldn't see me or speak to me ever again. He claimed that it was better for my sake and Fitz's if he locked himself away."

"What?" Abigail asked in shock. She found it difficult to believe that Merit could be so cold and unreasonable.

"I tried to tell him that Fitz was gone and I wanted, no, needed to see him," Lizzy continued, her breath catching with the frantic tenor of her words. "I said that it was only hurting me for him to pull away like he was doing but he wouldn't listen. He said he wouldn't see me because it would hurt Fitz and he was afraid he might hurt me next."

Abigail was transfixed by

the words. She stood very still, thinking over what Lizzy had said. It didn't make any sense. Why was Merit acting in such a way? Merit had always adored Lizzy, why was he pushing her away so cruelly?

"You have to help me. I don't know what to do," Lizzy urged.

"We will go and check up on Mr. Raleigh," Carlyle assured her.

Filled with shining relief, Lizzy turned and led the way to Merit's house with Carlyle and Abigail hurrying to keep up.

CHAPTER 19

Abigail was out of breath with exertion and worry by the time they reached Merit's estate. The structure loomed above them like a specter and Abigail felt queasy as she looked at the old house and wondered what was going on inside. Lizzy didn't hesitate to charge forward and demand entry. The disgruntled servant allowed them inside and then went about his business, ignoring their presence altogether. Lizzy went straight for Merit's bedroom and pounded on the door.

"Merit, let me in!" she demanded.

There was no response. Lizzy tried the doorknob and found it locked. Abigail's throat went dry with worry. Lizzy was sobbing as she called to Merit and begged him to let her inside. Carlyle approached Lizzy and gently laid a hand on her arm.

"Please, allow me to try, Miss Sutton," Carlyle said, pulling her away from the door.

Carlyle knocked firmly, a man's knock that demanded entry. No answer. Abigail could see the concern on Carlyle's face. His eyebrows drew together and his eyes were hard. "Mr. Raleigh, it's Mr. Carlyle, please open up," Carlyle called into the room.

There was a long, excruciatingly quiet moment before Merit, his voice quavering, responded. "I won't do it. I won't let you in."

It was the only response they received. Abigail and Lizzy continued to speak to him through the door. Carlyle continued to knock. But Merit refused to say anything more or even respond to any questions and demands from the others. The room beyond the door might as well have been empty.

Finally, Carlyle seemed to come to the end of his patience. He grumbled under his breath, "It's too dangerous for him to be alone."

Carlyle took a moment to consider what should be done next. He quit knocking at the door and took to pacing back and forth instead. Abigail watched him but before she could guess what he was planning, he moved. Carlyle threw all of his weight against the door to Merit's room, breaking it in with a resounding crack.

Lizzy yelped at the sudden

action, staggering back with hands raised defensively. Abigail looked inside the room and saw Merit standing with his eyes wide, shocked at Carlyle's sudden appearance. Both Lizzy and Merit had only seen the calm, collected side of Carlyle and so were surprised at his sudden reckless action. Abigail on the other hand, had seen Carlyle jump into a dangerous mire on two occasions and run into a burning munitions factory on another. She was momentarily caught off guard but not surprised.

Merit staggered back from his unwelcome visitors. His gaze looked clouded and distant to Abigail. Dark circles under his eyes told her that he hadn't slept for a while. His face was very pale, ghostlike, and with a thin sheen of sweat at his temples. His skin seemed stretched over his face, accentuating every angle and making him appear skeletal. He looked sick.

Lizzy rushed into the room towards Merit. Tears streamed freely down her face and her arms were open as if she meant to embrace the young man.

"Stay back!" Merit snapped at her.

Lizzy flinched as if she'd been slapped. Her eyes revealed great depths of hurt and pain.

"Keep her away from him," Carlyle quietly urged Abigail. He left no room for argument.

Abigail reached forward and grabbed Lizzy's arm. She gently pulled her friend back from Merit. The severity of Carlyle's words made Abigail wonder if her mentor feared that Merit might be dangerous. Abigail was starting to wonder the same thing. She was suddenly a little afraid of the young man she had called her friend. It didn't feel like the same

Merit she knew was standing in front of her now.

While Abigail held Lizzy back, Carlyle slowly approached Merit as if he were trying to calm a wild animal. Indeed, Merit didn't act unlike a feral beast. The whites of his eyes flashed, his nostrils flared slightly, and he looked ready to flee. Carlyle held up his hands placatingly.

"Mr. Raleigh, what is it that causes you so much distress?"

Merit blanched even further. Abigail wanted to rush towards him, afraid that he might pass out. Merit threw a furtive look toward Lizzy and Abigail. The expression clearly said that he didn't want to speak in front of them. Abigail was unwilling to leave.

When it was clear to Merit that Abigail and Lizzy weren't going anywhere, he leaned close to Carlyle and spoke quietly in an attempt to conceal his words from everyone else. Still, Abigail heard.

"I can't bear it any longer," Merit murmured. "It's all my fault."

Abigail wanted to yell at Merit until he accepted the truth that Fitz's death wasn't his doing. She wanted to persuade him any way she could that he wasn't guilty for Fitz's mistakes. Somehow she knew any words she spoke would be pointless.

After he had spoken, Merit seemed to sink into a trance of sorts. Carlyle said his name a few times to try to get his attention but Merit became unresponsive to anything any of them did or said.

"Lizzy, stay back," Abigail instructed her friend. When she was content that Lizzy was listening, Abigail released her friend's arm and approached Merit.

Abigail carefully laid a hand on Merit's forehead, checking his temperature. "He's running a fever," she announced. "He must be ill, likely as a result of all of the stress following Fitz's death."

Abigail considered Merit's condition and all of the symptoms he exhibited. His fever, his delirium, his bouts of anger. She wasn't sure what diagnosis to give but she was sure of one thing. "I want to keep an eye on him for a while. Someone should stay with Merit tonight; I don't think it's wise to leave him alone."

Even as Abigail spoke, Merit didn't pay attention to the words. It made Abigail even more nervous. With Carlyle's help, Abigail took Merit's arm and gently but firmly led him to the side of his bed. She forced him to sit and then she took one leg and Carlyle took the other, lifting until Merit was lying down on the bed, in the same foggy state of mind as before. It was like he had retreated in on himself.

"I'll stay here," Abigail

volunteered. "I want to keep an eye on his condition and see if I can find a diagnosis. I'll have to consult my textbooks to see if there's an illness that matches his symptoms, though it could be pure exhaustion I suppose."

"I'll stay too," Lizzy insisted. "I don't want to leave him."

Abigail was hesitant to accept Lizzy's help. She had a feeling that Lizzy's presence was at least in part responsible for Merit's fragile state of being and fits of anger. But Abigail also found that she didn't want to be alone with Merit. After weighing her options, Abigail nodded in acceptance of Lizzy's offer.

Lizzy took up a seat on the edge of the bed next to Merit, watching over him worriedly. Abigail took the opportunity to draw Carlyle into the hallways for a private word.

"I'm not quite sure what's

going on with Merit," Abigail confessed to her mentor. "But I'll find out and I'll find a way to help him."

"I suspect you'll have to find out what's going on with Miss Sutton as well," Carlyle said. "She's keeping something from us. Whatever it is, I believe that finding it out will be essential to solving this case and helping your friends."

Deep down, Abigail knew that Carlyle was right. Fortunately for her, she had a whole night with Lizzy and Merit ahead of her. She would get to the bottom of things if it was the last thing she did.

CHAPTER 20

Before Abigail rejoined Lizzy in the vigil at Merit's bedside, she made a stop at Stag Hall to inform her parents where she was spending the night and to gather a few things. Carlyle waited with Lizzy while Abigail returned home. Neither of them wanted to leave Lizzy and Merit alone. It saddened Abigail that Merit's behavior had made him unpredictable and perhaps even dangerous. Abigail dreaded the conversation that she must have with her parents before helping her friend but she also knew if she didn't tell her mother where she was, Mrs. Sinclair might very well call the police to search for her daughter.

Abigail found her mother right away when she returned to Stag Hall and with a deep breath explained the situation with Merit and the need to keep watch at his bedside.

"Should we send for a doctor?" Mrs. Sinclair asked.

"I am a doctor, or at least I will be one soon," Abigail responded shortly. "Besides, you wouldn't want anything to destroy the perfection of the neighborhood would you?"

Mrs. Sinclair lifted her chin defiantly. "You shouldn't be so bitter, Abigail. How can you think I'm so shallow? I am concerned about Merit. I'm sorry that it's come to this between us. I know we've never seen eye to eye and

I realize now that you truly hate me but I never meant to drive you away. I'm sorry."

Abigail turned away from the apology. She couldn't believe it, not really. Her mother was just trying to make her feel regret for her behavior and maybe Abigail did regret her words a little. She always saw the worst in her mother and read into every action as done out of selfish desires. That was one way in which Abigail knew she was the one in the wrong. However, after all of the ways her mother had hurt her and destroyed the trust between them, Abigail couldn't accept the apology.

"I do care for you, mother. I don't hate you. But I feel like nothing I do will be enough for my family. I can't condone your behavior either. You and Father have lived in sin for too long, drinking, partying, and having no care for anyone but yourselves. I cannot turn a blind eye to it now that I know better. I will *never* belong among the Sinclairs. I'm sorry that I've disappointed you and I'm sorry that things can't be different."

Frustrated, Abigail fled to her room before her mother could argue further. She closed the door behind her and sank to the floor against her bed. She didn't want to argue with her mother anymore but she was afraid that was one relationship that could never be mended. Abigail sighed and turned her head against the pink quilt that she hated so much. Out of the corner of her eye, she saw something lying under the bed. Abigail leaned down and reached for the object. It was her old anatomy textbook, her childhood treasure and what had inspired her love of medicine. She had always hidden it under her bed so her parents wouldn't confiscate it. When she had run away, she had been in such a hurry that she had forgotten it in its hiding place. She'd been devastated but unwilling to go back for it. Now, she picked it up and placed it on her bed. She would take it with her to Merit's. She had a feeling it would be a long sleepless night and she was eager to have the book with her to keep her occupied.

Abigail hurriedly packed a bag with some supplies and then snuck out before her mother or father could stop her again. She made the trek to Merit's home in the dimming light. She felt like her heart was dimming as well. Her hope was dwindling and the weight of being home drew her down more and more the longer she was there. When Abigail reached the estate and entered, she found Carlyle waiting in the hallway for her. A silent conversation passed between them.

"I'll be in one of the guest rooms," Carlyle told her.

"You're staying?" Abigail asked, unable to completely hide the hope from her voice.

Carlyle nodded and glanced at Merit's door, closed as much as possible after Carlyle had broken into the room. "He's yours and Miss Sutton's friend so I'll allow you two to care for him but I will not leave you alone in this house."

Abigail was grateful that Carlyle would be nearby. She only hoped his presence would turn out to be unnecessary. With a quiet knock on the door to Merit's room, Abigail entered and found Lizzy as she had left her, sitting on the edge of Merit's bed watching over him. Lizzy looked up when Abigail entered but then turned her gaze back to Merit. Abigail pulled up a chair and sat beside the bed. Merit, who had been sleeping, opened his eyes and gazed at Abigail with cloudy confusion.

"What are you doing here?" he asked with a raspy voice.

"You're sick, Merit. Lizzy and I are going to take care of you."

Merit blinked and looked almost relieved at the explanation. He gave a slight nod and then closed his eyes again, drifting off the sleep. Abigail watched the steady rise and fall of his chest. She took his temperature again and found that it seemed to have gone down but he looked no better than before. She sighed and settled back for a long night. Lizzy stood and stretched, pacing around the room before coming back and dragging a chair next to Merit's bed. She rested her cheek in her hand as she studied their friend.

"Do you think he'll be alright?" Lizzy asked in a whisper.

Abigail wasn't sure how to answer so she stayed silent. She

didn't want to lie to Lizzy. She wasn't sure what was going on with Merit but she did know one thing, he wasn't the same as he had been before and she doubted he could ever return to that version of himself.

As Lizzy watched Merit's calm sleep, Abigail pulled out Quinn's journal. The least she could do is get something productive accomplished. It was better than worrying. She flipped open the journal and began to read Quinn's next clue.

Entry 6:

With the Healer's retreat, the glass castle grew ever more fragile. The Queen Mother and the King's father raged at their daughter's escape. They focused all of their attention on the King who was starting to detest the position he had once held so dear. He found himself contesting with the Jester often. The Jester's parents were often absent from their estate, traveling to every destination of import and leaving their fool to his own devices. The Jester ruled his domain like a madman. He threw parties that rivaled any other. He drank to distraction and took his unpredictable temper out on any who dared warn him of his impending downfall. The King and the Poet tried to reason with him but to no avail. The Poet who was always such a gentle soul couldn't look at the Jester without coldness and despair in his eyes. It wasn't until the Heart's return that a spark of hope entered their lives. The Heart grew closer than ever before to the Jester. She unthawed his frozen heart and calmed his fiery temper. But only on occasion. Sometimes she experienced the worst of his torment. But her goodness was too great to hold it against him. She loved him and he loved her.

The King watched it all from afar, considering his own heart above all others. He spent many a night clutching the Healer's letter to his chest and pondering where he had gone wrong. It was during that time that he found another memento of her. Perhaps it was the very thing that had driven her away by instilling dangerous dreams into her overactive mind and causing her to refuse to settle for anything less than she desired. The King examined the artifact, a book. He had always thought its contents boring before but he had tried to be interested when he saw how much she adored what was contained within. He flipped to her favorite page and that was when it hit him like a terrible blow. He realized where the source of his troubles originated. Perhaps the most vital organ in him was toxic and corrupt. It needed repair that he was incapable of.

No man was capable of healing it once it was broken. Many months after that he found a solution, a Savior. Then his old life became unbearable and he knew he couldn't go back to the way things had been. He had to change everything about himself and become more like the Healer in many ways. Look to the Heart. Find it in a personal place where it was left last.

With a shock, Abigail realized that the next clue related to her anatomy textbook, the very textbook she had stumbled upon that afternoon and brought with her on a whim. Abigail nearly squealed with excitement at her good fortune. She drew the textbook out of her bag and laid it on her lap. Its heavy weight lent her comfort. 'Look to the Heart,' Quinn had instructed. Abigail thought it was as good a place to start as any. She flipped to the page in the textbook that discussed the anatomy of the human heart:

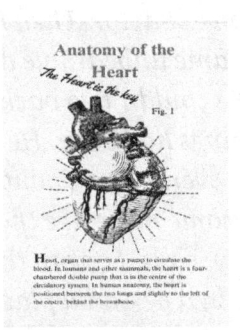

Anatomy of the Heart

The Heart is the key

Fig. 1

Heart, organ that serves as a pump to circulate the blood. In humans and other mammals, the heart is a four-chambered double pump that is in the centre of the circulatory system. In human anatomy, the heart is positioned between the two lungs and slightly to the left of the centre, behind the breastbone.

When Abigail opened the page two loose sheets of paper, a note and a letter, fell out onto her lap:

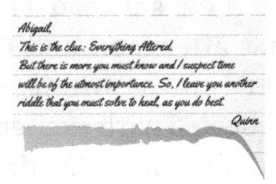

Abigail,
This is the clue: Everything Altered.
But there is more you must know and I suspect time will be of the utmost importance. So, I leave you another riddle that you must solve to heal, as you do best.

Quinn

> Abigail,
> The Heart is the key. I may have left but I can still see what is happening to my friends. You are the only one who can heal what has been broken. You've always had a gift for mending things. I want to help people too. I want to make amends with you. First, you have to help the others in the way I never could. It's too late for Fitz but not for Lizzy and Merit. Help them, see what they've been hiding, and bring it into the open.
> I'll see you soon,
> Quinn

Abigail read both clues and realized that while 'Everything Altered' was the two-word clue needed to solve Quinn's puzzle, there was a bigger mystery he wanted her to solve. He wanted Abigail to help their friends. To solve that particular mystery, 'The Heart is the Key'. Abigail glanced over the paper at Lizzy who was still leaning towards Merit, intently watching every breath he took. In all of Quinn's stories, Lizzy had been referred to as The Heart. Why was Lizzy so essential to get to the bottom of what was happening to Merit, what had happened to Fitz, and why Quinn had disappeared?

Abigail remembered Carlyle's earlier warning that she needed to find out what Lizzy was hiding from them to help Merit and solve the rest of the mystery. The more Abigail thought about it all, the more she realized that Lizzy was really at the center of everything. She was the reason Fitz and Quinn had fought. She was engaged to Fitz and everything had started to go wrong when she came to the neighborhood to live there all year. Whatever was going on, Lizzy was right at the center of it like she had always been at the center of things.

With that realization, Abigail felt that there was no time to waste.

"Lizzy, I know there's more to everything going on than you've been telling me and Carlyle. I need you to tell me everything. Tell me the truth," Abigail demanded.

Lizzy looked up warily and

her eyes revealed enough to know that Abigail's words had struck home. Perhaps without even realizing she was doing it, Lizzy reached for Merit's hand lying limp on top of his blankets. She entwined her fingers with his and Abigail realized the truth before Lizzy even spoke a word.

"The truth is, I'm in love with Merit," Lizzy explained.

Abigail felt her throat close but she stayed silent and listened.

"I told you before that I was going to break off the engagement with Fitz. It wasn't only because I didn't like Fitz's behavior. It was also because of Merit. I wanted to be with Merit. I kept putting off talking with Fitz because Merit didn't want to hurt his friend. To be honest, I did love Fitz too, or at least I had at one point. Merit tried to convince me that what I was feeling for him would pass and that I would be happier if I stayed with Fitz. Merit thought it would be better for everyone that way. I think he just wasn't willing to risk losing his friendship with Fitz or me. You know how he is, always trying to please others and protect them from pain. Fitz ruined everything."

Abigail wasn't sure how to react to Lizzy's words. She felt like she had known the truth all along but still been so blind to it.

"I thought that with Fitz dead, Merit would change his mind and want to be with me. But the opposite happened."

Lizzy's words unsettled Abigail. She wished Carlyle were there to hear the conversation and read between the lines. Could Lizzy have killed Fitz to get him out of the way so she could be with Merit instead?

"Everything is falling apart," Lizzy sobbed. "I don't know why Merit is acting so strange and I never wanted Fitz to end up dead. And now Quinn's gone too. You don't have to say anything, Abigail. I know it's shocking. I know that I've been a fool and my actions have hurt those around me. You're probably disgusted with me and maybe you'd be right to feel that way."

"I'm not disgusted, only surprised and confused," Abigail admitted. "I wish I had answers but now I only have more to think about."

Lizzy looked at Merit. "So do I."

The two girls passed the rest of the night in silence. They took turns dozing in their chairs and watching Merit as he slept. Abigail looked at the sleeping boy and wondered what must be going on in his head. She wondered why Merit had chosen to push Lizzy away after Fitz's death. Did he feel guilty for loving her when her fiancé met such a terrible end? It seemed like something Merit might think. Abigail would have to tell Carlyle everything she had learned. She hoped he would be able to find answers because she felt more in the dark than ever before.

CHAPTER 21

Early the next morning, Abigail left Lizzy with Merit and with Carlyle at her side headed home to solve Quincey's final clue. She was so close to the end of the mystery and she was desperate for answers. As she walked with Carlyle, Abigail told him about the conversation she'd had with Lizzy the previous night. Carlyle listened in silence and when Abigail had finished he still did not speak. Abigail could practically see the gears turning in his head.

"This is troubling indeed," Carlyle finally said. "It's worrisome but I believe we should solve Quincey's puzzle before we dwell too long on this new development."

Abigail couldn't agree more. She felt like the journal was burning a hole in her pocket. She knew if they could solve the puzzle, they would be one step closer to finding Quinn. The rest could wait for now.

When they reached Stag Hall, Abigail and Carlyle returned to the patio outside the ballroom and Abigail flipped open the journal to its final pages.

Entry 7:
The King may have undergone a transformation but his companions did not. Their misconduct and mania continued and accelerated. The Jester was uncontrollable. He had been left

alone in his house of vice. His parents were gone and his brother had left to serve in the battle of worlds. No one dared tell him that he was falling into folly and would soon be unable to escape. Even the Heart, who loved him, could not bear to rebuke his actions. The Poet was the most unwilling to push the Jester away. But the King found it more and more difficult to turn a blind eye to the Jester's actions and that of his parents the Queen Mother and his father. The lawlessness and selfish vanity were too much to persevere. One day, when the Jester was in a particularly foul passion, the Heart commented that he should be more like the Poet, calm, caring, and collected. The Jester in a fit of drunken anger struck out at the Heart and then the King had seen enough. When she left with tears in her eyes, the King stood his ground, grateful that the Heart and the Poet wouldn't be present to see what was about to occur. The King mustered his courage and confronted the Jester, demanding that he cease his hostilities, especially towards the Heart who had done nothing against him. The Jester responded harshly, claiming that the King was just jealous of his engagement to the Heart. He claimed that the King was in love with the Heart. But the King knew the truth and for once he was determined to speak his entire mind. He told the Jester that he was blind because it wasn't the King who loved the Heart but the Poet. The King warned the Jester that if he wasn't careful, then the Heart would leave him for the Poet. The Jester called the King's words a betrayal of their years of friendship and comradery. He claimed that the Poet would never betray him in such a way. The King knew that the Jester was correct and said as much. The Poet wouldn't betray his friend but what about the Heart? Would she continue to be so gentle when her future was on the line? The King further warned the Jester that the Poet was becoming unpredictable and although the man they knew would never turn on his friends, the new man whom the Poet was becoming just might. For the Poet was hurting and both the King and the Jester had done nothing to support him as they should as his friends. When the King said as much to the Jester, the Jester denied it and said that he had supported the Poet. The King claimed that the Jester was too selfish to see the troubles of anyone but himself. The Jester called the King judgmental and said he was too much like the Healer had been. The King took the intended insult as praise. He told the Jester that he would do well to be more like the Healer. He hoped that he had changed in such a way. He had changed and he could no longer turn a blind eye to what the Jester was doing. The Jester was destroying himself and all of those around him. The Jester was furious at the King's words and stormed away. It was later that the King heard the rest of the story, how the Jester had gone home and found his long-absent brother returned from duty and how his brother was determined to expel him from their home. The Jester fought against his fate and tried to injure his blood relation. When he failed, he ran to the only loyal friend he had left, the Poet. The Poet, in an attempt to distract the Jester from his troubles, suggested a walk on the cliffside. The Jester took the opportunity to fall back into his careless ways and as he strutted along the very edge, the rock gave way and he fell and fell far below where no one could attempt to save him again. The King heard the news and determined that there was nothing left for him in the glass kingdom. It had all fallen apart. He had one chance of escape, one that not even his parents had the power to revert. The day of his birth had come and gone and he had finally reached the age of accountability. He signed his name and left; the evidence lays at the place where everything ended. Icarus.

Abigail felt her heart hammering between her ribs as she finished reading the clue.

"'The evidence lays at the place where everything ended'," she quoted. "He must be talking about the cliffs."

"Then, it's time we returned to the cliffs," Carlyle said.

But before they could leave, a familiar figure rushed towards them, Lizzy. Abigail immediately knew that something was terribly wrong. She felt her heart stutter in her chest with despair and when Lizzy's terrified face came into view Abigail felt like her legs may refuse to support her.

"I tried to stop him," Lizzy exclaimed frantically, panting from her run. "I tried to make him stay but Merit ran away. I think he went to the Sawyer estate. He kept mumbling something that sounded like, 'Eric. Tell Eric.'"

Lizzy's words filled Abigail with dread. She looked at Carlyle who shared her troubled expression.

"Come, we must hurry," Carlyle urged.

He broke into a run, leading them towards the Sawyer estate and hopefully towards Merit as well.

Sure enough, they found Merit outside in the midst of what appeared to be a confrontation with Eric. Merit was kneeling before Eric, hands planted on the ground in front of him and head hung low.

"I did it," Merit exclaimed. "I killed Fitz!"

Merit was sobbing and spitting out the words with such certainty that it caught Abigail off guard. Lizzy turned pale and would have fainted if Carlyle hadn't caught her and carefully lowered her to the ground where she sat clutching her head. Abigail likewise felt off balance at the confession. It didn't make any sense. Surely Merit hadn't killed Fitz!

Eric Sawyer seemed just as unsure of what to make of the words as Abigail. Everyone thought of Merit as the innocent, reserved member of their group.

No one would suspect him of being capable of something as terrible as murder, especially not of his closest friend.

Merit was so sincere in his claim that Abigail saw Eric's face start to shift as he began to believe what Merit said.

"How dare you! How could you?" Eric questioned the prostrate figure before him.

When Merit didn't answer, Eric's expression changed from confusion and disbelief to anger. He kicked the kneeling Merit, sending him sprawling on the ground. Lizzy screamed and Abigail began to rush forward but Carlyle restrained her.

"Fitz was your friend!" Eric yelled at Merit.

"I was a monster," Merit added to Eric's insults. "I k…killed him. I deserve to die for what I've done."

There was so much agony

in Merit's voice that he sounded like an entirely different person. Abigail wished Quinn was there. Surely, he would have known what to do.

"Fitz was my brother!" Eric said, starting to get emotional. "I never even had a chance to make things right with him."

Eric took out all of his anger on Merit, throwing kicks at him as Merit did nothing to defend himself. Merit seemed to gladly accept the blows. After a moment, Carlyle rushed forward and pulled Eric back before he could hurt Merit any further.

The lack of attacks made Merit distraught. He staggered to his feet and rushed away. Abigail realized with mounting horror that he was running towards the cliffs.

"We have to stop him!" Abigail screamed.

She, Carlyle, Lizzy, and Eric

all ran after the runaway. Abigail ran perhaps faster than she ever had before. They caught up to Merit as he was standing on the edge of the cliff, only a few feet away from where Fitz had fallen.

"Mr. Raleigh, please step away from the edge," Carlyle said calmly.

Instead of heeding the warning, Merit took one step closer to the precipice.

Lizzy screamed. "Merit, get away from the edge!"

Abigail knew Merit wouldn't listen to anything any of them said. He was in a mania, she realized. His eyes were wild and unfocused, his breath frantic. He wasn't seeing them but something else.

"Fitz wants me to fall just like he fell," Merit said, his tone flat and certain.

"What do you see Mr. Raleigh?" Carlyle asked.

"I see Fitz standing behind you. He's gesturing to me, telling me to jump. I killed him. It's what I deserve. I led Fitz to the cliffs because I was jealous of him. I've always been jealous of him, especially because he and Lizzy were together. I put aside my desires for the sake of my friends and it ate me alive until I lost control and killed him. I must have killed him."

The strange words struck something inside Abigail and she came to a realization. "You didn't kill him," she told Merit. "What happened to Fitz was an accident, nothing more. There was no proof when Carlyle and I investigated the cliffside that anyone had tampered with the area. You were the only one who suspected foul play, Merit. Did you want Fitz dead?"

"Yes! No! I...I don't know."

"I don't think you did," Abigail answered for him. "You

were jealous maybe because of Lizzy and you wanted to be with her but you felt like you couldn't because it would hurt Fitz. But you were willing to sacrifice your happiness for theirs. When you talked with Carlyle, you struggled to remember what happened on the cliffside. You were trying to convince yourself that your hidden jealousy had led you to kill Fitz but no one killed him. He fell because of his own folly and there's nothing you could have done about it."

"No," Merit mumbled. "He told me I killed him."

Abigail's heart ached at the sincerity of Merit's words. Carlyle looked confused and Abigail realized that this particular area was more her expertise than his but he had been right all along in his assumption.

"Paranoia, auditory, and visual hallucinations, irritability, and confusion. You didn't kill him

Merit and Fitz isn't the one telling you that you did, it's you. Would I lie to you?"

Merit considered her question. Abigail's heart raced as she waited to see what he would do next. One step and he would fall. One breath and it could be his last.

"You wouldn't lie to me," Merit said. He hesitantly stepped away from the edge of the cliff.

Abigail released a breath of relief. Lizzy ran towards Merit and pulled him into an embrace. He stood frozen and allowed her to hold him but he didn't return the gesture. Eric, confused by everything wandered off as soon as Merit's fate was decided.

"I'll expect an explanation for all of this later," Eric murmured to Carlyle as he left.

Carlyle approached Merit. "Let's get you back to your home, Mr. Raleigh," Carlyle said kindly.

Before she followed after

them, Abigail searched the cliffside until she found a small box hidden behind some rocks. She opened it and inside found the final clue.

Conscription papers with Quincey's name and information. It didn't require a detective to decipher where her brother had gone.

"Oh, Quincey," Abigail murmured, clutching the papers to her chest.

She didn't have time to dwell on them. Stuck to the back of the paper was another note left by Quinn, the final piece of the clue, written on an old newspaper clipping.

THE WORDS LEFT BEHIND

> ...most ny, or
> way.
> ...ay Longville
> ...d car park (GR
> with map. "GP"
> ...ome of thou and
> ...hen sound the
> you meet a sign
> ...ead, half right.
> ... to (in quick
> ...otpath and over
> ...oint; do not cross.
>
> *"Nobody*
>
> ...bridge. There is
> ...is southern bank.

The clue left a sour taste in Abigail's mouth. '= Nobody', something about it didn't sit right with her. She would have to solve the riddle later. First, she had to help Merit.

CHAPTER 22

Abigail knew that what she had to do next would be very difficult. She found herself praying to Carlyle's God, a God that she still wasn't entirely sure she believed in but she had been seeking more and more for guidance and help. Then, with a deep breath, Abigail entered Merit's office. He was slouched in a chair. He looked exhausted and there was an animal-like fear in his eyes. He watched Abigail approach as if she were a predator about to attack. Abigail faltered. How could this poor, wretched man before her be her childhood friend? How had things gotten so bad?

Carlyle patted her shoulder reassuringly. "I'll be right here, Miss Abigail. Do what you must."

Abigail sighed. There was no other option. She had to tell Merit the truth and help him in any way she could. Abigail sank into the chair across from Merit and leaned towards him, trying to make herself seem as non-threatening as possible. Lizzy who was kneeling beside Merit's chair gave Abigail a grateful look.

"Abigail," Merit said, a hint of clarity returning to his eyes. "What's going on? I don't understand…"

After a moment's hesitation, Abigail reached out and lightly touched Merit's hand. It was cold and shaking. "We need to talk, Merit, about everything."

He nodded and Abigail saw

a hint of the boy she used to know in his expression. It gave her the courage to continue.

"Fitz is dead and gone. He's never coming back."

Merit flinched at the words. "But I saw him. I heard him."

"I know you have but they've been nothing more than auditory and visual hallucinations. Have you ever experienced something like that before Fitz's death?"

Merit was silent for a long moment. He looked away from Abigail with eyes closed and mouth twisted as if he were in pain. Finally, he said one simple word that broke Abigail's heart a little further. "Yes."

"Merit, you need to be honest with me about your symptoms because I want to help you and I'm afraid. I don't want to do anything that will hurt you. I don't want to make a mistake."

"I know you want to help but I don't think you can. I've heard things for a long time now, things I know can't be real. When I was a child I used to hear my mother's voice long after she was dead. I would hear it on the breeze as if she were calling to me. I would hear her singing. Sometimes I even thought I saw a flash of a dress turning down the hall. It all got worse when I went to boarding school. My mother's singing turned into taunts. Sometimes I thought I saw her face but it was cruel and hidden in shadow. I wrote about it in my poems. I didn't think something was *wrong.* I thought being in a different place just made me have waking nightmares of sorts."

"And then you started seeing and hearing Fitz after he died?"

Merit clutched his head. "I heard his screams as he fell. It kept me up at night and haunted me during the day. I saw him laughing and raging as he always did but it was worse, so much worse. He was fragmented like a ghost. He kept telling me that it was my fault, that I had always wanted him dead. It was real. He had to have been real. I can't be imagining it!"

Abigail squeezed his hand until he looked at her. "Just because you're imagining it doesn't mean it isn't incredibly real to you. None of us think you're lying, Merit."

"But you think I'm crazy, don't you?"

"You're not crazy," Carlyle interjected. "You have been through a great deal of pain and heartache, Mr. Raleigh. Those things leave a mark. You are still in pain. You are still suffering. We only want to help you be at peace."

Merit shook his head. "I... I don't know what to do."

He started to shake and Lizzy

rose to hold him in an embrace. This time he didn't push her away. He rested his head on her shoulder and shook with silent sobs. Abigail saw that he wasn't only pained at the knowledge that something was wrong, but he was also afraid. She saw a hint of relief on his face as well, relief that there was an explanation for all of the horrible things he had experienced.

"What's wrong with me?" Merit asked.

"I hesitate to make any kind of diagnosis when this isn't my field of study," Abigail warned him, "but I believe you have a genetic predisposition that has revealed itself during a time of great trauma, first with the death of your mother and now more potently with Fitz's death. I believe you're experiencing schizophrenic episodes, Merit."

Abigail dreaded saying the words. She knew that sometimes a

diagnosis made things seem more hopeless than they were. She didn't want to hurt Merit and she was afraid her words would only add to his pain. However, she was surprised to find that he accepted her diagnosis calmly. He nodded and didn't argue. Perhaps he had suspected for some time that things weren't right and it was a relief to finally have answers.

"Whatever is going on, Merit, you won't be alone," Lizzy said, her voice stronger than Abigail had ever heard. "I'm going to be here to help you through it. I love you and I want to help."

Merit shook his head. "I can't let you do that, Lizzy. I don't want to hurt you any more than I already have."

"Don't you understand? It only hurts me more when you drive me away. I know it won't be easy and I won't expect more than you can give but I also won't give up hope that things can get better."

"We will find you the help you need," Abigail reassured her friend. "And Lizzy's right. You don't have to do it alone."

Merit, exhausted from his struggles, nodded, ready to accept their help. Abigail released a breath of relief. She knew that it was only the beginning of the trial. There was much that would have to be done and Abigail would need to consult someone more experienced than herself to verify her diagnosis and ensure Merit received the treatment he needed. In the meantime, there was one other problem that had to be solved.

"Merit, I told you that we would help you, now I'm asking you to help me. I've followed the last clue in Quinn's journal but now that I have all of the clues, I have to solve his riddle. You know I've never been great with words but you are. Maybe you can help."

Merit perked up, eager to see the puzzle and force his mind to different matters of interest. Abigail had already read the final entry of Quinn's journal and she handed the book to Merit so he could read it as well.

Entry 8:
Abigail, I trust that you've discovered all of the clues I left for you. You've always had a mind keen for learning and that won't rest until you've found the answers you seek. Now, it's time for you to solve the riddle. You might need some help for that. Perhaps, look at the assets around you. You'll need an eye that has an intimate understanding of words and their meanings. Oh, and one other thing, you'll need clue #2. Use this code to find the words you require: 1A2A, 1B2B, 1C2C, 1D2D, 1E2E, 1F2F, 1G2G. Fill in the blanks. The last

THE WORDS LEFT BEHIND

five lines require letters from the clues. Clue #2 will fill in the rest.

*Abigail, with_ _ I will _ _ nor _ _ _ _.
My True _ was _. My _ _ was _erly, _
_ a _ _. _ _ _ I _ that _ _ _ _ in the _ I _
and I _ _. Then _ _ with _ _ and _ _. I
_ to _. My _ _ _ that of a _. _ _ _ _ _*

Good hunting.

Abigail suspected that Quinn had always wanted her to seek Merit's help for the last part of the riddle. They both knew that Merit was the one who had a way with words. He was the one who could form majestic ideas with nothing more than a pen and paper. Abigail watched as Merit studied the final entry and the clue. She had included the two-word clues that Quinn had forced her to find on a sheet of paper:

1. Franklin Sinclair
2. Ike Aaron
3. North Northeast

4. Dangerous Future
5. My Remorse
6. Altered Everything
7. Equals Nobody

She had also included Merit's poem, clue #2.

"I think I can solve it," Merit told her. He reached for a pen and hovered his hand over the page. "1A2A, 1B2B, etc. is a rhyme scheme. That must be referring to the lines of the poem. I used an ABAB CDCD EFEF GG rhyme scheme or the rhyme scheme of a sonnet."

"What poem are you talking about?" Lizzy asked.

Merit took a deep breath and began to recite it:

Never can beauty compare
nor a good nature surpass
Imperial; nowt impaired
Eternal; our good compass

Treading evil; good, trod towards
When you made us realize

*painful lies sow new discord,
life shifted to idealized*

*Was your smile our lives reborn?
Commenced to end all conflict
mother's kindness; never shown
scorn
Fathers we had before, but strict*

*Longed we always to escape
life's ill pains; we sought your
shape*

When Merit had finished his recitation he said, "I wrote it for you, Lizzy. I never got the chance to give it to you and then I was too cowardly to do so."

"It's beautiful," Lizzy said with tears in her eyes. "Thank you."

Abigail cleared her throat. "So, how does the poem fit into Quinn's clue?"

Merit turned his attention back to the paper. "The first line of the poem is line A then the second is line B and then A again and B again. Quinn's clue is 1A2A which I think means he wants you to use the rhyming words from each line. So, line 1A would be 'Never' and 'Compare'. Line 2A would be 'Nor' and 'Surpass'. The same is true with lines 1B and 2B and the rest."

Merit wrote each of the words down next to Abigail's numbered list, creating a second numbered list beside the first:

1. Never Compare
2. Nor Surpass
3. Imperial Impaired
4. Eternal Compass
5. Treading Towards
6. When Realized
7. Painful Discord
8. Life Idealized
9. Was Reborn
10. Commenced Conflict
11. Mother Scorn
12. Father Strict
13. Longed Escape
14. Life's Shape

Abigail stared at the list and felt

even more confused than before. "If these words are added, it just makes a scramble. There's no solving this. What was Quinn thinking?"

"It's why he warned you that you would need the help of someone with a way with words," Merit told her. "It *is* a scramble. That's the point. You have to unscramble the words to make a coherent sentence. That's what poetry is. You take meaningful, resonant words and compose a story with them. Using the other clues you've gathered, I think I can understand what Quinn was trying to say. It will just take some trial and error."

With impressed amazement, Abigail watched Merit set to work deciphering the clue. He used the scrap of paper to try multiple combinations of words, moving them around like pawns on a chessboard.

Finally, with a smile, Merit said, "I've got it."

Abigail leaned close to peer over his shoulder at the completed sentence:

Abigail, with <u>Franklin</u> <u>Sinclair</u> I will <u>never</u> <u>compare</u> <u>nor</u> <u>surpass</u> <u>imperial</u> <u>Ike</u> <u>Aaron</u>. My True North was <u>impaired</u>. My <u>eternal</u> <u>compass</u> was <u>Northeasterly</u>, <u>treading</u> <u>towards</u> a <u>dangerous</u> <u>future</u>. <u>My</u> <u>remorse</u> <u>when</u> I <u>realized</u> that <u>painful</u> <u>discord</u> <u>altered</u> <u>everything</u> in the <u>life</u> I <u>idealized</u> and I <u>was</u> <u>reborn</u>. Then <u>commenced</u> <u>conflict</u> with <u>mother</u> <u>scorn</u> and <u>father</u> <u>strict</u>. I <u>longed</u> to <u>escape</u>. My <u>life's</u> <u>shape</u> <u>equals</u> that of a <u>nobody</u>.

"But it still doesn't tell me where Quinn is," Abigail exclaimed in frustration. After so much work, she still didn't know where her brother had run off to.

"There's one more part of

the riddle to solve," Merit pointed out. "Quinn's note said 'The last five lines require letters from the clues. I think we have to take the first letter of each of the two-word clues you found and use them to create new words."

Merit did as he had suggested and composed another jumble of letters.

"This is ridiculous!" Abigail said, throwing her hands in the air.

"Just wait. It's another scramble," Merit responded, quickly reorganizing the letters. "There! The first word in each two-word set is the first half of the sentence while the second word is the second half. And now we know where to find Quinn."

Abigail stared at the last part of the riddle, finally in front of her after so long.

Find me = San Fran

"Well," Carlyle said, "it appears we are going to San Francisco."

CHAPTER 23

The train ride to San Francisco gave Abigail plenty of time to think over everything that had happened in the last few days. She thought of Merit and Lizzy and Fitz, her old friends, one dead, one changed, and the other annoyingly the same. She thought of the home she had left behind and the pain of returning there even briefly. She wondered if she would ever make peace with her parents and if such a thing were even possible

Carlyle had agreed to join

her in the final leg of their journey to find Quinn. He sat across from her on the train, silent and contemplative. Although they had solved the mystery of Fitz's death and Quinn's disappearance, Abigail felt far from satisfied. She felt more distraught than ever. She at least knew that Quinn hadn't killed Fitz, no one had. But the truth was perhaps more painful. Quinn was leaving to fight in the war. The conscription papers were proof enough of that. And Merit's underlying illness was what had caused such suspicion and dread in him.

As the train jostled along, Abigail's mind returned to a past conversation she'd had with Carlyle. She had asked him how he could believe in God when there was so much pain and evil in the world. Abigail thought she understood the truth now. In the midst of her pain at being in her old home surrounded by friends who were changed, confronted by the death of a past companion and the disappearance of her brother, she had sought comfort in a higher power, a God who had a plan greater than her own. Science was no comfort or consolation. Abigail had believed before she realized. When she had started to read the Bible that Carlyle had given her, she'd come to accept that God was real and all powerful but it had taken her reaching a personal rock bottom, being reminded of her past and her complete inability to do things on her own, to turn to Him. Now, Abigail wasn't entirely sure what to do next. She wanted to discuss it with Carlyle but she couldn't find the words and instead sat in silence as the scenery rolled past the moving train.

    She hadn't told her parents where she was going or that she had found Quinn. She wanted to talk to her brother before her parents got the chance. Abigail needed to make amends with him and set things right, especially before he left for the war. He had run away from their home just as she had. She was certain that he would have told their parents where he was going if he had meant for them to find him. He had left the journal for *her* to find, no one else. Abigail had written a letter to her parents and she would mail it as soon as she reached San Francisco. It would give her a few days head start before they followed after her.

Despite Abigail's mixed feelings and concerns and Carlyle's contemplations, there were brief moments of conversation as the train rolled ever onward. They discussed what had taken place and the mystery they had solved.

"I must admit that I was impressed with your brother's

clues," Carlyle said. "Quincey Sinclair must be a very bright young man."

"Yes. I'm glad the search is over. If not for Merit, I never would have been able to solve that riddle. I just hope that we won't reach San Francisco and discover that we're too late. What if Quincey is already gone?"

"I have a feeling that you will be right on time," Carlyle assured her.

They arrived in San Francisco weary from their travels but with a renewed energy now that the end of their mystery was in sight. Abigail inquired among the recruitment offices until she learned that Quincey Sinclair was stationed at the shipyards with a contingent of soldiers preparing to ship out. With bated breath and a pounding heart, Abigail followed the directions, looking for her brother.

She peered at the great vessels lined up for war, the soldiers wishing farewell to family and friends, some for the last time. Abigail could hardly breathe as she scanned the ranks for Quincey. At last, she found a familiar face. For a moment, she couldn't move. What if he hadn't wanted her to find him? What if he had made the riddle confusing in the hopes that she would give up and abandon the search for him? What if he hadn't changed and he despised her for the letter she had written to him so long ago? There were too many 'what ifs'. Abigail felt sick with the uncertainty flooding her chest.

"Go to him," Carlyle encouraged her.

The words were the final push she needed. Abigail ran to her brother, calling his name with tears in her eyes.

Quincey turned and his face lit up when he recognized her. He opened his arms and she fell into his warm embrace. Abigail buried her face in his shoulder and held him tight.

"Oh, Quincey!" Abigail exclaimed, afraid if she let him go he might disappear.

Quincey held her just as tight as if he were afraid of the same thing. "I missed you, Abigail."

After a long moment, Abigail pulled away, taking in the sight of her brother in his uniform.

"Do you like it?" he asked her, a hint of humor in his voice. "I hear men who die in the Navy at least die clean."

"Why are you going, Quinn? Father could have found a way for you to stay here."

"That's exactly why I'm going. I'm tired of living by a different set of rules from everyone else. As soon as they lowered the draft age, I volunteered, regardless of what Father would have done to prevent it. That's why I ran away. I have a duty to God and country and fight for what I hold dear. But I'm glad *you* found me, Abigail. I've missed you. There's so much I've wanted to say to you. I was wrong about so much. I was selfish and cruel just like our parents and I hurt you. I never meant to hurt you or anyone else."

"I said some harsh things in that letter I left you," Abigail said. "I'm sorry too."

"Everything you said, I deserved and it was because of that letter that I discovered how desperately I needed to change. Your letter drove me to find the truth, to find God."

Abigail was startled at Quinn's words. "God?" Abigail asked her brother.

Quinn nodded. "I was hopeless. I felt that everything in life had lost its meaning. After the incident at the boarding school when one of Fitz's pranks went too far, I was disgusted at myself and the life I lived. I knew something had to change I just didn't know how. When you left it awakened something in me. I started searching for answers and I stumbled across a Bible sitting in our family library. I remembered going to church on Easter and Christmas as a child and something rekindled inside my heart. I read the Bible and realized that the salvation promised within was what I was searching for. After accepting Christ, I became even more determined to change. I was filled with a desire to serve others. I thought serving my country was as good a place to start as any."

"I just can't believe you disappeared so suddenly," Abigail said, shaking her head.

Quinn laughed. "I only did the same as you had before."

"It looked bad that you

disappeared right after Fitz's death," Carlyle interjected. "As a detective, I've witnessed many innocents who were convicted because of unintentionally guilty actions."

"A detective!" Quincey exclaimed. "I didn't think my disappearance would cause enough fuss for mother and father to hire a professional to track me down."

"This is Detective Carlyle, my mentor. I've been conducting a medical internship under his guidance," Abigail explained. "When Mother showed up to tell me you had disappeared, Carlyle volunteered his services to help track you down. Little did we realize we would have another mystery to solve when we arrived."

"Fitz," Quincey murmured. "Please, tell me what happened with Merit and Lizzy?"

"It's not good. Merit has been

having hallucinations. I'm going to find help for him but I only pray it will be enough."

"I suspected something like that," Quinn admitted. "When we were at boarding school, I began to notice how strangely he was acting. He was more anxious than ever and he started to display a temper. He rarely slept and seemed to be in a trance-like state at times. I regret that I was so preoccupied with my worries that I didn't help him in the way I should have."

"He's not alone," Abigail said. "I'll help him and so will Lizzy."

"Thank you, Abigail. You have no idea how worried I've been about them. Merit and Lizzy are the only reason I hesitated to leave home. I didn't want to abandon them. But I knew I had to leave. I knew you would help them in a way I never could. And thank you, Mr. Carlyle, for helping my sister find me and help Merit and Lizzy."

Carlyle nodded. "Your sister has helped me on more than one occasion. Besides, it was enjoyable to follow your clues. I believe you would make a fine detective yourself, Mr. Sinclair."

Quinn smiled. "I think I'd like that in another life but for now I've found my duty. I'm sorry to leave, Abigail. I hope you'll accept one piece of advice from me, despite my many faults. Believe. I know that you've always been a skeptic, a scientist. But there are greater things than we could ever fully understand. There is a God who created this universe and crafted us for a purpose."

"I know," Abigail said softly. "I've changed too, Quincey. I've been putting off accepting the truth for a while now because I was afraid to turn away from what I've always believed but Mr. Carlyle, my studies, and finally reaching the bottom of my abilities, I've discovered that what I've always doubted is really the only thing that I *can* believe. It's the only reasonable explanation for a universe filled with such wondrous miracles. And working with Carlyle has shown me how pitiful humans are when left to their own devices, how pitiful I am. I can only rely on the blood of Christ, it's the only hope I have for salvation. I'm ready to accept that now."

Quincey pulled her into another hug, holding her tight. When he pulled away his joyful expression was replaced with sorrow.

"I have to go now," he told her. "I don't want to say goodbye so I'll just say, 'I'll see you again'."

Abigail felt tears spring to her eyes. She fought the emotion back with a valiant effort.

"We both have a duty to help others," Quincey reminded her. "Out duties just come in different forms. I'll do everything in my power to return to you, Abigail. Pray for me when I'm gone?"

Abigail nodded with teary eyes. "I will. Be safe, Quinn. Goodbye."

Quinn waved a last farewell before turning to join the other sailors. Abigail watched him go with a mixture of sorrow and joy. She hated to see him leave but she was so grateful that they had both found their path in life and for once it seemed that their paths had converged once again.

"Let's go back home," Abigail told Carlyle. "I've had enough mystery for now. I'll be happy to return to blessed boredom for the moment."

CHAPTER 24

Before they left San Francisco, Abigail mailed the letter to her parents. She felt a sense of finality as she did so. The letter explained where she had found Quincey and his plan to fight in the war. It also said in plain terms that Abigail had no intention of returning home. Perhaps someday she would reconcile with her parents and find peace in her old home but for now, she only wanted distance between them. She likewise mailed a letter to Eric

Sawyer, slipping the Sawyer family ring between the pages to return to its rightful owner. She gave him only a brief explanation of what they had discovered about Fitz's death and urged him to not take out his anger on Merit. She felt that she owed him no more than that.

When she arrived back in Chicago with Carlyle, she released a breath of relief. The feeling of freedom was almost overpowering. However, there was still work to be done and her relief was somewhat short-lived. She still had a promise to uphold. She still had to find help for Merit. It took everything in Abigail to suck up her pride and go to the one place she knew she would find answers regarding Merit's situation.

Doctor Hastings.

Carlyle's former assistant, a young somewhat stuck-up doctor was no easy man to talk to and Abigail hated to admit any sort of weakness in front of him. She felt that she had much to prove where he was concerned. She had to prove that even though she was a woman, she was more than capable of becoming a doctor. However, she also respected Hastings's seniority and expertise. Abigail wouldn't take any chances in helping her friend. She was willing to put aside her pride and seek a second opinion to ensure Merit received the best treatment for his illness.

She went to Hastings's office, a small facility positioned at the front of his home, alone to seek his advice. She knew bringing Carlyle would only make Hastings more difficult to deal with. When he answered the door, he appeared surprised and when she explained the reason for her visit, the expression turned to one of smug superiority. Abigail inwardly groaned. However, Hastings quickly took on a demeanor of professionalism. Abigail knew at heart, underneath his disagreeable exterior, he truly did want to help people. Abigail took his seasoned advice and sent a telegram to Lizzy that recommended different treatment options for Merit to consider.

"He's your friend, this Merit Raleigh?" Hastings asked her.

Abigail nodded. "A childhood friend. He's someone very dear to me. That's part of the reason I came to you for another opinion. I can't handle the issue from an entirely impartial point of view."

"I understand. Considering our past disagreements, I'm surprised that you sought *me* out."

"As much as I hate to admit it, I trust your judgment," Abigail said truthfully.

Hastings smirked.

"Don't get a big head," she berated. "There were simply no

better options."

"I'll take that as a compliment. I do hope that your friend finds peace."

"Me too. I feel like maybe I've finally found the peace that I've been searching for."

Hastings studied her long and hard. His look was not cruel or judgmental as was sometimes the case. Instead, he looked at her with grudging respect and maybe even compassion. Abigail thanked him and fled as quickly as possible, somewhat unsettled by the strange look.

She was relieved to be back in Chicago and back to the regular boredom of Carlyle's office. The little apartment was more a home to her than her real one was and she was eager to settle back into routine. She spent her free hours studying the Bible Carlyle had given her with a new view of the matter. Now that she had come to accept God, she saw the Bible in a new light. It was in the dark of her room, all alone as she had done many things in her life, that she accepted God officially into her heart. She repented for her sins, her pride, and her desire to put intellect above all else. She asked God to help her unbelief because she still had doubts and she still wanted answers. But she didn't need all of the answers immediately. She knew the most important things. God had sent His Son Christ to die for her sins and the sins of the world. She was hopeless without that abundant mercy. She knew she could do nothing on her own and must rely on Him. She knew that God was all-powerful and all-knowing and that He had a plan for her whether she understood it or not. A realization occurred to her that just as an infection had to be killed before new, good bacteria could make the body healthy, so too did she have to kill her old self and abandon her old ways before she could gain an understanding of God's will and His ways.

If one good thing had come from the trials of the last case it was that Abigail had finally realized that she couldn't do things on her own by her power. She couldn't live by her own laurels. She wondered what the next mystery she and Carlyle would face would be. She hoped it would turn out to be far less personal. She was surprised at her change of heart in more ways than one. She couldn't imagine what it would have been like for her if she'd conducted her internship anywhere else. There was nothing else she wanted to do now other than solve cases, uncover mysteries, and help people in any way she could. Maybe her journey had taken a slightly different path from what she'd originally expected but maybe that was okay. Maybe it was all according to design.

Attention!

If you've made it this far, then first of all, thank you! I truly hope you've enjoyed this book.

If you want to read more of my stories, check out the *Forest Dwellers* series, *Eden's Last Stand*, and the *Ademar Duology* also available on Amazon.

Also, please consider leaving a review of this book. Reviews help independently published authors like me more than you can imagine.

If you would like to learn more about me and my writing, please check out my website: https://

sgmorand.com or follow me on social media at: sgmorand or S.G. Morand.

ACKNOWLEDGEMENT

This book wouldn't have been possible without the help of my mother who works tirelessly to edit my books and looks for any loose threads throughout mysteries like this one, my dad who helps touch up the books covers and ensures that everything looks its best, and all of the family and friends who encourage me to keep writing, buy my books, and show their support in any way they can. Wow was that was a run-on sentence. The point is, it takes a lot of help to bring a book to print, and I couldn't do it without everyone who supports me. I want to give a special thanks to my friends who I met at Bible school while I was working on this book. My fellow writers who encouraged me to keep pushing forward whenever I felt like I had hit a roadblock, who got excited about my stories, and shared their own stories with me. I so enjoyed writing with you all and getting to know you. Thank you Joy for sharing your story with me and inviting me into your world and for listening while I talked through hiccups in my plot. You also motivated me to work on my project whenever I looked over and saw you typing away. Thank you Grace for getting so excited about Eden's Last Stand and for offering to make artwork for my characters. I can't wait to read your story soon. Thank you Ava for keeping me accountable on all of the medical aspects in my writing (don't look too closely at the plausibility in this book) and for being so inspiring, what you do reminds me to keep striving for more. And Ella, thank you so much for having writing clubs with me. I miss our coffeeshop talks and writing sessions. Thanks for sharing your many stories and helping me push outside my comfort zone in my own writing. It was awesome to rant about book ideas with you. The next book will be dedicated to you. You all brought new life to my writing journey. Thank you.

ABOUT THE AUTHOR

S. G. Morand

Sarah Morand lives in Montana where she loves archery, collecting sarcastic t-shirts, and her obnoxious rat terrier, Ivan. She has an eclectic taste in books and her ideal house would be a Victorian library. Sarah started writing in middle school and after writing a plethora of short stories, finished her first novel by her senior year of high school. She is the author of the Forest Dwellers series,

Eden's Last Stand, and the Ademar Duology available on Amazon.

Find more information at:
sgmorand.com
And follow on social media at:
Instagram: sgmorand
Tiktok: sgmorand
Facebook: S. G. Morand - Author
Goodreads: S. G. Morand

BOOKS BY THIS AUTHOR

Forest Dwellers: The Exile

Traitors, Banished, Exiled...
After her father and many others are unjustly banished from the dukedom of Mac'tire, Brier's life changes forever. The hardships of exile force the outcasts to plead with the duke to allow them to return. Along with four other teenagers, Brier is tasked with journeying back to Mac'tire. Brier's trust in God is put to the test. She must overcome her fear of past failures to guide her friends. But the journey back to Mac'tire won't

be as easy as they thought.

Forest Dwellers: The Battle Of Mac'tire

Brier and her friends have barely survived the grueling journey to their old home, the dukedom of Mac'tire. Their faith in God and each other has been put to the test. Now they'll face their greatest challenge, gaining an audience with the duke and clearing their names. Beneath the surface are undercurrents of corruption, misplaced trust, and an impending coup. The teens not only must prove their parents' innocence, they must navigate the palace intrigue to save the dukedom. But, their worst enemy might prove to be each other.

Forest Dwellers: The Wolves Of Lupus

Abducted...

After completing their training as foresters, Brier and Reid return to Mac'tire for some much-needed rest. Unfortunately, leisure will have to wait. Soon after they arrive, Flint goes missing. The prime suspect behind his disappearance is a dead man. Brier and her friends must hasten to the Dukedom of Lupus in order to rescue Flint and confront an unexpected threat. Opposition encroaches from all sides as they battle not only present foes but the past as well. They will have to rely on God and each other to save their friend and themselves.

Forest Dwellers: Trials Of The Trade Route

Pressure, Perseverance, Penance... The young outcasts have finally settled into their new lives, but their trials are far from over. Brier and Reid are sent to investigate a strange cabin in the forest that might hold the key to resolving current trouble and uncovering secrets of the past.

Meanwhile, Flint and Erin deal with their own troubles in Lupus. Duke William wants to give Corvus's son, Lyall, a second chance. But can he be trusted?

Lance has his own adventures as he works with a group of vigilantes to resolve a series of vicious attacks on Mac'tire's newly established trade route with Lupus. A new threat has arisen that might prove more dangerous than Corvus himself.

The former outcasts are drawn into a series of mysteries and perils as they strive to uncover the secrets of the past, protect the present, and ensure a bright future for the dukedoms. Will the new challenges they face prove too much for them, or will it bring them closer to God and each other?

Forest Dwellers: A Poisonous Past

Past... Present... Future
Brier and her friends have come far since they returned from exile. As they've settled into their new lives, they thought they had put their past behind them. With Tan wreaking havoc on the trade route, Lyall's motives in question, and the discovery of a long-lost document hiding a shocking truth, they are all forced to look back before they can move forward. They won't have long to dwell on their troubles. Danger lurks just around the corner and the consequences could be disastrous. Will they overcome the past in time to save their futures?

Forest Dwellers: Tales Of

Mac'tire

Tales of Mac'tire is a thrilling collection of never-before-seen short stories, novellas, and deleted scenes from the Forest Dwellers series. The novellas explore the dreaded exile that spurred Brier and her friends into action and dives into the backstories of the Forest Dwellers villains. A collection of short stories explores the wide cast of characters like never before and deleted scenes and bonus information give an inside look into how the series was created.

Eden's Last Stand

On an island ruled by a corrupt regime, a series of dangerous and immoral experiments force an underground group of Christians to make a desperate stand. Kidnapped on their way home from school, Lynn and Lex are thrown into the middle of a battle between the forces of tyranny and Eden, a group of rebels who operate in the shadows. When Lynn becomes the target of sinister experiments conducted by the forces controlling the island's precious resources, the once-distant struggle becomes personal. Eden's warriors are former victims, each just as determined as Lynn to expose the evil around them and put an end to their suffering. Equipped with unique abilities, Eden's outcasts struggle to control their powers and harness them for the good of all. Will this ragtag group be able to put the past aside, follow God's will, and bring about a brighter future, or will they succumb to the dark forces arrayed against them?

To Turn The Tides Of War

A Kingdom in Peril, A Reluctant Hero, and a Convergence of Darkness...

Corin Faye wants nothing more than to be a knight for the kingdom of Ashnah. He's just an orphan from a backwater mountain town, barely able to lift a sword. God has greater plans in store for him. When it is discovered that Corin possesses magical, God-given gifts, he is whisked away to the capital city of Castille to serve the king and train as a mage. While Corin battles with his destiny, a war rages on the border of Ashnah. The wicked kingdom of Freiwade has a dangerous weapon, a foe that Corin will be hard-pressed to face.

A story of intrigue, deceit, and faith, the Ademar Duology follows Corin and a wide array of characters as they battle dark forces to protect what they hold most dear. The Ademar Duology is an epic fantasy adventure with a focus on Christian principles and ideals.

The Lost Heir

Conflict among the three kingdoms has reached a fever pitch. After years of brutal rule, the wicked kingdom of Freiwade has driven the Skellan people to the brink of rebellion. One shortcoming has kept the seaside kingdom from regaining its independence. There is no one to lead them. With rumors of a Lost Heir to the Skellan throne circulating, Corin, Ruena, and Finch set out in search of an ally to quell Freiwade's reign once and for all. They aren't the only ones hunting for the Lost Heir. Dane, the illegitimate son of the old king of Freiwade has fled his home for fear of his life. He seeks answers and a way to save his kingdom. He seeks the Lost Heir. The spies of Ashnah have another mission, to rescue Cal and to determine whether the new king of Freiwade can be trusted. They must go to new lengths to achieve their goal and face dangerous secrets of the past that will test their trust in each other and themselves. However, the greatest threat to be faced is one not created by any man.

A story of intrigue, deceit, and faith, the Ademar Duology follows Corin and a wide array of characters as they battle dark forces to protect what they hold most dear. The Ademar Duology is an epic fantasy adventure with a focus on Christian principles and ideals.

A Mire Of Secrets

1941 Chicago.
A war rages, a body is found

drowned in the muddy mire of the Chicago Harbor, and a young medical student is faced with a dilemma. Abigail Sinclair must complete an internship to gain her license as a doctor. When her best friend is sent overseas as a field surgeon, Abigail is faced with the much less appealing position of serving as assistant to Detective Carlyle, a strange private detective with unorthodox methods. What originally promises to be a boring and unproductive internship quickly takes a turn for the sinister when a man is found drowned in the harbor. The only suspect: a ghostly woman apparition. Amongst a plot to quell a union uprising, the unsolved mystery of a nearly identical murder, arson, and Carlyle's half-truths and secrets, Abigail realizes that her internship is the least of her worries. A mystery beckons and she must solve it, there's simply no other choice.